"You'd better go, Halley."

Mark's words were sharp, punctuated with small gasps as he tried to get his breathing under control.

Bewildered, stunned by the abrupt ending of his kiss, Halley stumbled back. "What happened?"

"Nothing," he blurted.

"Not from where I'm standing." She grabbed his arm. Anger gave her the strength to whip him around. "Was this another one of your little tests? I failed the one in the elevator...and the one in the pediatrics ward. Were you testing me to see if charm could get me into your bed?"

"You said you'd leave if I told you to go. I'm telling you. Go!" He gripped her arms, heading her toward the door. "We'll both be better off."

Halley dug her heels into the carpet, resisting the pull of his hands. Realization of what had happened struck her. She'd seen too much, gotten too close. His hands trembled, a dead giveaway of his inner turmoil.

"You're scared, aren't you?" she demanded as he hustled her toward the door. "What are you afraid of?"

Dear Reader,

Spellbinders! That's what we're striving for. The editors at Silhouette are determined to capture your imagination and win your heart with every single book we publish. Each month, six Special Editions are chosen with *you* in mind.

Our authors are our inspiration. Writers such as Nora Roberts, Tracy Sinclair, Kathleen Eagle, Carole Halston and Linda Howard—to name but a few—are masters at creating endearing characters and heartrending love stories. Their characters are everyday people—just like you and me—whose lives have been touched by love, whose dreams and desires suddenly come true!

So find a cozy, quiet place to read, and create your own special moment with a Silhouette Special Edition.

Sincerely,

The Editors
SILHOUETTE BOOKS

JO ANN ALGERMISSEN
Purple Diamonds

Silhouette Special Edition

Published by Silhouette Books New York

America's Publisher of Contemporary Romance

SILHOUETTE BOOKS
300 East 42nd St., New York, N.Y. 10017

Copyright © 1987 by Jo Ann Algermissen

ISBN: 0-373-09374-8

First Silhouette Books printing April 1987

All the characters in this book are fictitious. Any
resemblance to actual persons, living or dead, is
purely coincidental.

Books by Jo Ann Algermissen

Silhouette Desire

Naughty, but Nice #246
Challenge the Fates #276
Serendipity Samantha #300
Hank's Woman #318

Silhouette Special Edition

Purple Diamonds #374

JO ANN ALGERMISSEN

believes in love, be it romantic love, sibling love, parental love or love of books. She's given and received them all. Ms. Algermissen and her husband of twenty years live on Kiawah Island in South Carolina with their two children, a weimaraner and three horses. She considers herself one lucky lady. Jo Ann also writes under the pseudonym Anna Hudson.

Chapter One

"Halley Twain? On the pediatric floor?" Dr. Mark Abraham's snort of disbelief clearly indicated his opinion of the transfer request the floor supervisor held in her hand.

"She's qualified," Nurse Chaney stated unequivocally. She respected Dr. Abraham's surgical expertise, but she was in charge of the pediatric ward's nursing staff. "Her evaluations are excellent."

"Let me see them." Mark quickly scanned the application. Dark brown hair. Blue eyes. Five foot one. One hundred and eight pounds. Twenty-eight years of age. No medical problems. Registered nurse with a bachelor of science degree from St. Louis University. He examined the form with one dark eyebrow raised. The succinct description could have fit many of the nurses at St. Michael's 250-bed, private hospital.

He silently took note of the glowing praise from Halley Twain's current supervisor. The nursing service appraisal form rated nurses on a scale from one to ten. Nurse Twain averaged a nine. Close to, but not quite perfect. On the lines allowed for additional remarks, handwritten comments extolled her capabilities, calling her caring, conscientious, capable. These three C's were what he considered essential for anyone working with his patients. Too bad the form lacked spaces for a character analysis, he mused. From what he'd heard from an intern, Halley went beyond *C* to *D*: deceitful, disruptive . . . and desirable.

Mark swallowed, clearing the bitter taste from his mouth. Handing the forms across the counter, he said, "Personally, for whatever my opinion is worth, I'm opposed to the transfer."

Martha Chaney poked her wire-framed glasses snugly against the bridge of her nose. "Why?"

"I've seen her type. Beautiful . . . and knows it. She performs well in a fast-paced environment, but she'll find the routineness of pediatrics boring. Six months from now, she'll request another transfer." His dark eyes narrowed slightly. "Or she'll latch on to another intern who isn't as perceptive as Jason Malone."

"Her vita does indicate a tendency to job-hop. She's worked in several hospitals during the past five years," she replied, ignoring his flip remark about one of her least favorite interns. She thumped the résumé with the knuckle of her middle finger, chuckling to herself. Of all the doctors at St. Michael's Hospital, the last person she expected to notice how a woman looked was Dr. Abraham. "Now that you mention it, she is striking. Interested?"

"Hardly," Mark scoffed. His ex-wife, Cleo, had taught him to be wary of beauty, of women who moved into life's fast lane by bedazzling some unsuspecting sucker into marriage. Now, medicine was his wife, his mistress, his love. He was satisfied with his current single status. "Burn victims seldom play with matches a second time."

"Halley Twain reminds you of Cleo?" Old enough to be the good doctor's mother, Nurse Chaney asked questions that others wouldn't dare to ask. "It's been years since Cleo worked here, but I didn't notice any physical resemblance between the two women."

"They may not look alike, but they're the same type." He seldom repeated things he'd heard, but the thought of being in daily contact with Halley Twain loosened his tongue. "Dr. Malone called her a cross between a barracuda and an alley cat…sleek and shiny on the outside, but with a mouth and claws that could rip a man to shreds. She nearly ruined Malone's medical career by insisting that he work all day and party all night."

"Gossiping, Doctor?" Nurse Chaney asked sarcastically. "Oscar would be ashamed of you."

A faint tinge of red rose from beneath his white collar. "Oscar is a dummy."

"So is a doctor who gets tangled up in the hospital grapevine. If anything, I feel more comfortable knowing she's no longer associated with Dr. Malone."

"Agreed. He was lucky to escape, wasn't he?" Mark asked, smiling grimly as he twisted the meaning of her words.

Martha's chin jutted forward. She slowly shook her head. As floor supervisor, she relied on the accuracy of the hospital's assessment forms. Rumor and speculation about a nurse's private life seldom influenced her decision. Reliable, efficient nurses were difficult to find.

"I don't trust kitty-'cudas with my kids. Do me a favor. Keep Halley Twain away from my patients unless absolutely necessary if you decide to accept her on your floor."

Martha glanced over her shoulder. "Is there a sign on my back that says, 'Make Nurse Chaney's day by asking for a special favor'? You know we'll be understaffed during the holidays so I can't make any promises. Speaking of Thanksgiving, can we count on you and Oscar to entertain the patients?"

"Oscar would never forgive me if I kept him locked in his trunk during the festivities. I've been working on some magical stunts that the kids will love." Mark leaned across the Formica countertop and whispered, "Care to be the lady who bravely climbs into the box and serenely smiles as I jab swords—"

Martha gasped in mock horror. "Your reputation precedes you, Doctor. You're renowned for your accuracy with a surgical instrument."

"And I'm accurate about Nurse Twain, too," he retorted glibly, drawing her back to the original topic of conversation. "She's more of an illusionist than I am."

A blinking light caught their attention.

Groaning, Nurse Chaney moved from behind the desk. "Tony Miller's light. I swear, I'd hire Halley Twain in a minute if she could weave some sort of magical spell around Tony's thumb to keep it off the call button. He's set a new record for complaints.''

"Daniel Edwards's patient?''

"Uh-huh.''

"Anything I can do?'' He joined her as she stepped around the edge of the counter.

"Nothing ethical.'' Her voice dropped to a whisper as they approached Tony's open door. "He's scared and angry and lonely, but that doesn't cure his hemophilia or justify his complaints.''

"This is his third visit to the hospital since last summer, isn't it?''

Nurse Chaney nodded. "And it won't be his last. He's a daredevil! Would you believe he tried out for a neighborhood football team last fall? He's in here now because of a nasty fall he took while playing ice hockey.''

Mark sympathized with Tony. They could control the pain caused by hemarthrosis, joint bleeding, but not Tony's desire to be a normal, healthy boy. He glanced toward the smoking lounge. "Is his mother here?''

"No.''

A look of relief passed between them. Tony's mother treated the nursing staff with the same condescending manner he felt certain she used on the servants in her home. Each time Tony left the hospital his mother stopped by the nurses' station to comment about the service her son had received. Nothing made the short hairs on a nurse's neck stand on end quicker than equating nursing with servitude.

"I'll be in Judy's room if you need me," Mark offered, continuing down the corridor when his companion turned into Tony's room.

Mark silently chastised himself for speaking bluntly about the Twain woman's request for transfer. He trusted Martha's ability to pick and choose her staff with utmost care. A noncommittal shrug from him would have sufficed.

Feigning indifference had been impossible once he'd read the complimentary comments on Halley's evaluation sheets. It ticked him off. Jason Malone's evaluation had suffered greatly because of her. Mark had lost track of the number of times Jason had arrived on duty late, bleary-eyed, but he vividly remembered Jason's excuses. Invariably they began with, "Halley wanted to go . . ." and ended with, "Who can sleep with a woman like Halley sharing my bed?"

Mark's memories of dragging himself to work after one of Cleo's social outings made him more lenient than he should have been with the young intern. By the end of Jason's three-month stint in pediatrics, Mark had been thoroughly sick of hearing about Halley Twain's virtues and flaws. He wasn't about to let Nurse Twain sink her claws into another intern. He'd said what he had to say to prevent that from recurring.

"Preventive medicine," he argued aloud. "Far more effective than treating another wounded intern."

Nevertheless, Mark could have kicked himself for breaking his self-imposed, ironclad rule against repeating tales. His policy had earned him the reputation of being aloof. That didn't bother him. He preferred it. Few people dared to question him about his private life.

"Dr. Abraham? Is that you?" Judy Gadsworth asked, touching the remote control button and switching off her television.

"Um-hmm." A warm smile curved his lips. "You should be sound asleep, little princess."

"What about you? Don't doctors need sleep?" She scooted to the side of the bed, patting the covers with one pudgy hand. Mark heard the rustle of paper between the sheets. The eight-year-old's eyes held a look of dismay. She forgot about her questions and stammered, "Uh, I only had a nibble off one, uh, peppermint. The girl next door had a whole box of them."

"Sue isn't a diabetic."

Judy grinned. "I won't tell her I'm a diabetic if you won't."

Mark shook his head tolerantly and held out his hand. "No candy."

"No lecture?" Judy bargained, reaching under the sheet. She pulled out a half-eaten mint wrapped in sticky cellophane. She glanced at the plastic wastepaper container, raised her hand and sighed as she released the sugary treat. "Other kids get candy when they're in the hospital. All I get are oranges. I hate oranges. I'd like to stab them with needles."

Mark realized being different from other children was a source of frustration for Judy. Bending at the waist, he removed the plastic bag inside the waste can, then straightened. "Where'd you stash the rest of them?"

"Me, hide candy? Don't be silly!" Judy batted her eyes innocently. Seeing that her ploy wasn't working, she sighed and dug deeper beneath the sheets. She dropped five more pieces into the bag he held. "That's all of them."

"You know how you'd feel tomorrow if you'd eaten these tonight, don't you?"

"Yeah. But, Dr. Abraham, I have a sweet tooth—" her thumb and forefinger spread a good three inches apart "—this big!"

"What happened to those sugar-free candies your parents bought?"

"They're yucky. My sweet tooth isn't going to be fooled by imitation candy. It wants the real McCoy."

Mark flashed her one of his rare smiles that he reserved for children. At eight, Judy was already able to wrap the opposite sex around her little finger. He teased, "Maybe you need a dentist more than a pediatrician. The tooth fairy ought to pay plenty for a tooth that big, Princess."

Judy giggled. "Can't put it under my pillow. A huge tooth under my pillow would keep me awake all night. You know how important it is for me to get my sleep, don't you?" She faked a yawn.

Mark tucked her sheet under her chin, alert for the fruity odor symptomatic of ketoacidosis. This late at night her drowsiness was normal. Her respiration appeared normal. Mark winked. "Sweet dreams, little princess."

"Sleep tight. Don't let the flu bugs bite." She tried to return his wink, but both eyelids closed instead of only one.

Her alteration of the quip, sleep tight and don't let the bedbugs bite, tickled Mark as much as her attempt to wink. Judy was an irresistible imp despite her illness. "I'll see you tomorrow."

Mark quietly moved to the door, into the corridor. He recognized Tony Miller's voice shouting, "I hate you, you old battle-ax! You're supposed to take my blood pressure, not use that thing like a tire pump. Whaddaya think I am? A flat tire?"

Unfastening the Velcro, Martha tried to ignore the tirade. She made a quick notation on his chart, then set a paper cup on the nightstand. Tony knew what she expected without her asking. Hospital routine hadn't changed since the last time he'd been there.

"Where'd you get your nursing diploma? Out of a Cracker Jack box?"

Martha Chaney bit her lip to keep from responding angrily. His constant complaining combined with his tantrums made caring for him difficult. Nurses were human. Tony's discomfort made him forgetful of that fact.

"What's the problem, Tony?" Mark demanded, his voice stern.

Tony pointed one accusing finger toward Nurse Chaney. "She's the problem. That she-devil and her assistant demons enjoy ordering me around. Nobody, but nobody tells Tony Miller when to—"

Mark made a slicing motion with his hand. "That's enough, young man."

Regaining her composure, Martha said, "I expect a specimen first thing in the morning."

The boy's chin thrust forward belligerently. Slowly and deliberately he picked up the cup and squeezed his fingers closed. His final spiteful act had Martha Chaney grinding her teeth in anger. Tony tossed the crumpled paper against the wall. Mark heard her quick intake of air. The glint in her eye signaled her impulse to commit mayhem. Ready to mediate if necessary, Mark inched closer.

"We'll discuss it in the morning," Martha said, controlling herself admirably. Her soothing voice concealed her justifiable anger. "I know you're uncomfortable. I'll instruct the nurses making morning rounds to be careful of your elbows."

Her kindness took the steam right out of Tony. He slumped against the pillows. For a moment, the way his chin wobbled, Mark thought the boy was going to cry.

"G'night, Tony." Nurse Chaney motioned for Mark to precede her from the room.

Once they were out of hearing distance, Mark said, "You handled that situation very well."

"For a second there, he almost had me. He's too sick to be violent, so his wicked tongue does the dirty work for him."

"Do you think Halley Twain could have handled him as well?"

Martha smiled. "We'll have to wait and see, won't we?"

Groaning, Mark realized that he'd pushed Martha too far. Halley Twain's application for transfer would be approved.

Two weeks later, Halley consciously straightened her shoulders to keep them from sagging. She'd worked her eleven-to-seven shift in the emergency room, and started in pediatrics on the seven-to-three shift. Ideally, back-to-back shifts rarely occurred. Her transfer necessitated this exception.

She'd barely had time to change from her white uniform into apple green slacks with a matching over-blouse. Informal attire was permitted on the pediatric ward. The pleasant, professional smile she'd worn all day felt as stiff as the starched nurse's cap adorning her short, dark curly hair.

The first day on a new floor is never easy, she reminded herself, lengthening her stride as she headed toward the elevator on her way home.

Having trained in pediatric nursing, Halley hadn't been surprised to find that she never really liked the hustle and bustle in the emergency room. But when she'd first come to St. Michael's that had been the only available position. Pediatric nurses tended to hold on to their jobs longer than nurses in other wards. Openings were rare. When Halley had heard a pediatric nurse was quitting to get married, she'd eagerly filled out a transfer application. Another six months of working in ER and she'd have become a nursing burnout statistic.

Changing wards was preferable to changing hospitals. She'd applied for a transfer and within days had been notified that she was accepted.

At first she'd jumped for joy. But during the weeks she'd spent familiarizing the new ER nurse with procedures and the monitoring equipment, she'd fluctuated between anticipation and dread.

Her off hours were spent blindly completing her routine chores while debating the wisdom of making another change in her life. Whether fixing meals, cooking, washing, ironing or cleaning house, she was preoccupied with a bad case of indecision.

Maybe she was taking on more than she could handle. Maybe she couldn't play the role she was hired to play. Maybe she should have moved on to another hospital rather than moving within the hospital. Although she detested not knowing what happened to the patients who left ER, maybe she wouldn't be able to handle working on the pediatric floor either. Maybe caring for severely ill children would demand what remained of her emotional reservoir.

Recalling her doubts, Halley shook her head. Physical, mental and emotional exhaustion had to be better than being on the receiving end of sympathetic smiles from her co-workers in the emergency room. Five months had passed since Jason Malone had completed his internship and left St. Michael's Hospital—and Halley—behind.

The all too familiar story had tugged at the heartstrings of the other nurses. Even nurses who'd initially been standoffish toward Halley had been distressed. Everyone had treated her as though she'd been suffering from an incurable, terminal illness.

She'd made the right decision. Her legs ached from being on her feet fourteen hours, but her inner satisfaction dulled the ache. She loved her new job.

By noon, the sinking sensation in the pit of her stomach caused by meeting the nursing staff and doctors had diminished. If any of them knew about her relationship with Jason Malone, they were tactful enough not to comment on it.

Oh, she'd seen a few of the young nurses eye her up and down like a potential competitor for the doctors' personal attention. Years ago, she'd probably have done the same thing. In an occupation filled with attractive women, jealousy wasn't uncommon, but age and experience and an advanced degree from the school of hard knocks had changed Halley's perspective. Involvement with any man, especially a doctor, was not on her priority list.

Her main task for the day had been to familiarize herself with the ward. Mentally she constructed a map. The head nurse's office was on the left, across from the family sitting room. Private and semiprivate rooms lined both sides of the corridor with the nurses' station squarely in the center. Behind the reception desk were four computers where information regarding each patient's illness and medical treatment was constantly updated. A circular stand held patients' charts. A door led to the conference room that also served as the nurses' lounge. Another door led to the drug room. Familiarizing herself with the placement of the emergency equipment, and medicines stored in the cabinets and refrigerator was essential and time-consuming. She'd briefly checked out the clean utility room for sheets and pillowcases, and the dirty utility room for soiled linens.

Time was her worst enemy. She'd vaguely familiarized herself with everything, placed names with faces, found out who did what, performed her routine duties with the patients, recorded her observations for the nurses on the next shift, when she'd been reminded that three o'clock had arrived. Tired though she was, she'd made one last tour through the nurses' station. She had to be as familiar with the station as she was with her apartment. Nurses didn't have time to fumble around, looking for equipment. Everything had to be at their fingertips.

Halley pressed the elevator's Down button. Lost in thought, she barely noticed the man in green scrubs waiting for the elevator. An inane thought, born from fatigue, brought on a wan smile. She'd come up in the world. The emergency room was on the first floor, pediatrics on the third.

The elevator's bell rang. Halley glanced above the stainless-steel door at the red lit arrow that pointed downward. She shifted her bulky coat, and impatiently waited for the doors to open.

Both Halley and the doctor started into the elevator at the same time.

"Excuse me," she muttered, halting midstep when the color of the scrub uniform caught her attention. Hospital etiquette dictated who had the right of way: the doctor. As in the military world she'd been brought up in, rank had privileges. Once inside, she recognized the hawklike profile of Dr. Mark Abraham, pediatric surgeon, and moved to the panel of buttons. She asked politely, "Which floor?"

"Sixth."

The doors closed before she could exit and wait for the other elevator. Great, Halley thought, arching one foot to relieve the aching muscle in her leg. Tempted to point out the original direction of the elevator, she let her hand hover over the button marked G. Hard as she tried, she couldn't keep her professional smile from slipping into a grimace as she touched the six.

"You were on the wrong floor, weren't you?"

Halley turned sideways to face Dr. Abraham. He isn't exactly handsome, she mused, wondering what feminine instinct made her want to step closer. Tall and lanky aptly described him. An unruly lock of dark hair covered the scowl on his wide forehead. Eyes, even darker than his hair, openly stared at her puzzled expression. From what she'd heard while working in ER, there wasn't a nurse in the hospital who hadn't set her cap for him. From the day she first came to St. Michael's she'd heard about what a fine physician he was. That had to be the reason for her sudden urge to narrow the gap between them.

"No, sir," she replied, surprised and a bit flattered that he recognized her. She smiled happily. "I transferred from emergency care to pediatrics. My name is Halley Twain."

"Halley? Rhyming with alley?"

"Yes, sir." Her smile died a quick death before it reached her eyes. "That's Twain. Rhymes with sane."

"Umm," he replied, letting his doubt hum in her ears.

The animosity he'd felt when Martha Chaney approved Halley's transfer request faded as Mark noticed that her eyes were a violet color, not blue. The faintly hurt, quizzical look he saw in them temporarily knocked him off guard. He wondered if those dark curls could cling to a man's hand as easily as they nestled against her cap. Fingers itching, he lowered his steady gaze to her lips. Her lipstick had worn off, leaving them bare and somehow vulnerable looking.

A hard knot coiled in his stomach. Instantly he recognized the nearly forgotten symptom of being physically attracted to a woman.

Get away from her, he told himself. Remember what she did to Jason. Barracuda. She's dangerous!

Halley shifted from one foot to the other. Idle conversation? she wondered. Did he rhyme names with words to help him remember them? Or had she made some terrible faux pas? Should she have offered her hand? She wiped her hand along the side seam of her uniform. Not the way they've started to perspire, she silently answered. His eyes seemed reluctant as they followed the course of her hand. A nervous hiccup lodged in her throat as his dark eyes intensely studied her.

What does he think I am? Some kind of mutant virus he's put under a high-powered microscope? She squirmed under his close scrutiny. Her pulse fluttered wildly at the base of her slender neck.

When the uncomfortable silence had become unbearable, Mark said in a flat voice, "Pediatrics must be boring for someone used to being in the fast lane."

"I beg your pardon." Her heart slammed against her ribs. She'd evidently flunked whatever test he'd given her. She had occasionally encountered silent hostility from women when she first met them, but never from a man. Usually her appearance generated quite the opposite effect.

"I said..." Mark paused, sighing heavily at her obtuseness.

"I heard what you said, but I'm not certain I know exactly what you mean."

Shooting her a you're-beautiful-but-dumb glance, he paced his explanation as though speaking to a not-too-bright two-year-old. "Pediatrics takes patience."

His insinuation was as clear as the angry red splotches staining her cheeks. Just who did he think he was? She owed him the professional courtesy of let-

ting him enter the elevator first, but being a surgeon
didn't give him the right to whittle on her character
without benefit of a local anesthetic.

"Exactly what makes you think I'm impatient?"
she demanded, forgetting who he was and what position he held at the hospital.

"You can hardly wait to get out of the hospital.
Deny that you wanted to punch the ground-floor button, if you can."

Yes, she wanted to go home. She'd been at St. Michael's for sixteen straight hours. She was exhausted.
Struggling to keep a lid on her temper she hesitantly
replied, "Yes, but..."

A bell chimed and the elevator stopped. Dr. Mark
Abraham stepped through the opening doors like
Moses parting the Red Sea. No backward glance. No
goodbye. Nothing.

"Round one?" Halley muttered, feeling soundly
defeated as she touched the ground floor button, then
leaned against the wall. Her stomach lurched as the
bottom seemed to fall out of the elevator.

That was the wonderful pediatrician Jason had
raved about? He was the man whose bedside manner
Jason had practiced in front of the mirror? The nurses
she'd met today practically worshiped the ground he
walked on. Were there two doctors at St. Michael's
named Mark Abraham?

Befuddled, Halley mentally replayed what had been
said. She'd informed him of her transfer, introduced
herself, then wham, verbal war had been declared.
Nothing about her pleased him: not her name, not her
occupation, not even her appearance. He'd stared at
her intently, but there hadn't been an appreciative

gleam in his eyes. If anything, he'd acted as if he wished she'd get out of his sight forever.

There had to be some sane explanation. Perhaps his day had been even rougher than hers. She remembered Jason saying how involved Dr. Abraham became with his patients. Perhaps an operation that morning hadn't gone well. One of his patients could have taken a turn for the worse. Maybe...

By the time Halley stepped from the elevator and headed toward the revolving door, she'd convinced herself that his antagonistic behavior must have some logical explanation.

What am I doing? she asked herself as she stopped in front of the ceiling-to-floor windows lining the front of the hospital. She slipped into the fleece-lined trench coat she'd carried draped over her arm. Was she actually making excuses for a man she barely knew? He could have had a great day and was celebrating by making everyone around him miserable!

Her thoughts had come full circle. She'd blamed him for being rude, then blamed herself for being insensitive; now she was back to blaming him for being rude. For a woman who earlier proclaimed that her last name rhymed with sane, her logic was decidedly muddled.

Halley hunched her shoulders, bracing herself for a wintry blast of air as she pushed against the door. One thing was certain, she was going to keep her distance from Dr. Mark Abraham. Whatever the reasons for his behavior, she wasn't about to become another man's whipping boy. With that decision firmly implanted in her mind, she glared up toward the sixth floor, then briskly strode toward the bus stop.

Mark stood in the atrium on the sixth floor and watched the lone feminine figure trudge away from the hospital. She'd fallen into his verbal trap, but he wasn't proud of himself. In fact, he'd spent the past few minutes wondering how he was going to apologize to her.

Twice within the past few weeks he'd let his mouth overload his brain. Both times Halley Twain had been the cause. He'd ridden in that same elevator hundreds of times with other nurses. Why hadn't he politely nodded and appeared preoccupied the way he routinely did?

Because the instant she'd smiled, your stomach somersaulted, he ruefully admitted.

He'd been around hospitals long enough to know people reacted in different ways to pain. Some were stoically silent, others bellowed. Some cried, others laughed. Only a thin veneer of civilized behavior had kept him from beating his chest to divert the pain he felt from zeroing in on his heart. Savage, primitive instincts had goaded him to protect himself from her charm. He'd been calm, cool and downright mean. He'd verbally slapped her while every cell in his body had been screaming for another of her sunny smiles.

Did she smile at all men the way she'd smiled at him?

The light from over his shoulder and the darkness from outside the window turned the plate glass into a shadowy mirror. He studied himself, not liking what he saw. There had been another time, another place, where he'd reached the same conclusion.

His eyes closed as he allowed a memory to claim him. From out of the past he could almost hear Cleo's sultry, deriding voice. They'd been getting dressed to go to one of Cleo's social functions. Seated in front of the vanity mirror, she had brushed her long, auburn hair. A satisfied gleam in her golden eyes had told him she knew exactly how he'd rather spend the evening.

"You're sure we have to go to this party?" he'd asked, preferring to stay at home and relax.

"We're expected to attend these charity shindigs. You may not enjoy them, but I do." Exasperated by his reluctance, she'd tossed the brush on the vanity table. "For heaven's sake, Mark, why do you think I married you?"

His hand had stilled, leaving his tie slightly askew. He'd asked himself similar questions from the moment they'd met. Why had such a vivacious woman encouraged him? Why had his slightest touch sparked passion in her before they married, and why had she turned so cold afterward? Why had she married him?

His throat closed. He couldn't ask.

Cleo's slender arm gestured from the mirror to Mark. "Take a long, hard look at yourself. I know what *you* see, the eminent Dr. Mark Abraham, healer of sick and injured children." She paused, fluffing her hair. "Know what *I* see? Bags under your bloodshot eyes, stooped shoulders, a little pouch under your belt from eating that starchy hospital food. Believe me, I didn't marry you because you're a fine specimen of a man."

Wounded, but still standing, he whispered, "Why, Cleo? Why did you marry me? Was it for children?"

Her responding laughter had been high, shrill.

"My, my, my, Mark. You've developed a peculiar sense of humor." She turned, boldly facing him.

"Status and money, my dear. I expected you to give me everything I couldn't afford on a nurse's meager salary. Frankly, you don't have enough money to make me want your child. Who'd raise it? You? You're married to St. Michael's. Be content with those snotty-nosed brats at the hospital. They may not look like you, but that in itself is a blessing."

Cleo went to the party alone. He'd been physically ill.

Six weeks later, Cleo left . . . permanently. Another doctor, older, wealthier, escorted her from party to party. On rare occasions over the following years, their paths crossed.

His medical expertise should have taught him that unless a wound is fatal, the patient heals. Cleo's cutting remarks had injured him, but not fatally. Gradually his emotional wounds healed. His scars were barely noticeable.

Several months ago he'd seen his ex-wife and been mildly surprised when he realized she could no longer hurt him. There was no pain, no anger, no nothing. He'd actually felt sorry for the man she was leading around by the nose.

Mark had thought he'd completely recovered. What a laugh! He'd known how similar Cleo and Halley Twain were. Yet within ten seconds of meeting her he'd wanted her.

Mark's clenched fist struck the inch-thick hospital window. He welcomed the pain shooting from his knuckles to his shoulder. Eyes squeezed tightly, he forced the unpleasant memories of Cleo back into the dark recesses of his mind.

Grimacing, he looked downward. The bus had come and gone, taking Halley with it. He knew where she lived. Hellcats had a permanent address. Halley Twain could go to hell, but she wouldn't take him with her.

Chapter Two

By eight o'clock the next morning, Halley was prepared for early-morning doctor rounds—or so she
thought. The morning routine of listening to taped
reports by nurses on the eleven-to-seven shift, check-
ing patients' vital signs and dispensing medication had
been completed.

Doctors began to arrive and Halley was able to
match up faces with familiar names on the charts. She
made mental notes as she unobtrusively observed the
length of time each doctor spent with a patient. Like
nurses, doctors were responsible for far more than
dispensing medication. Keenly aware of the importance of emotional support, Halley despised what she
privately called "three-minute eggheads." Eggheads
rapidly glanced over the patient's chart, announced
any changes in orders and hustled to the next patient.

They had cash registers for hearts. From what she could observe, St. Michael's was blessed with no egg-heads.

Opening Jimmy Owens's chart, Halley skimmed his lab reports. The prognosis wasn't good. Without a kidney transplant, he'd be in real trouble. She instantly recognized Dr. Abraham's cramped writing. A handwriting expert would have a ball with this, she thought sarcastically. Although the letters were clearly legible, they were tiny. She had to squint to read them.

"You'll get used to it."

Halley glanced up at the small name tag hanging on a bright pink blouse and from there to Jill Matthews's friendly face. Attractive, tall, blond and blue-eyed, Jill seemed the perfect California beauty. Only her Missouri twang gave her true origins away.

"Dr. Abraham gives me goose bumps," Jill added.

Assuming Jill had received the same cold-shoulder treatment Halley had received in the elevator, Halley nodded her head in benign agreement. New to the pediatric wing, she refrained from adding to the other nurse's opinion.

Tammy O'Brian, the unit clerk in charge of the computer, overhearing Jill's remark, rolled her chair back and asked, "Drooling over Dr. Abraham again? Martha Chaney has a better chance with him than you do."

Reassessing the cause of Jill's goose bumps, Halley was glad she'd kept her mouth shut.

"She's at least thirty years older than he is," Jill grumbled. "Chaney and the kids are the only people he smiles at. I'd pay a week's salary for one of those smiles."

Tammy took the chart from Halley's hands. "Find a kidney match for Jimmy Owens and he'd probably give you a smile . . . and a hug."

"I'd donate both of mine if I thought it would get me anywhere. At least he doesn't ignore you." Jill's eyes raked over Tammy's mousy-brown hair and pale complexion. "What's your secret?"

"Charm. Intelligence. Wit." Tammy arched her back, defining her plump curves.

"And married?"

"That, too," Tammy agreed. "Uh-oh. Speaking of Nurse Chaney . . ." She rolled her chair back into position behind the computer.

"Dr. Abraham needs assistance changing a bandage in 317." Martha directed her order toward Halley. "Jill, set up the medication tray, please."

Why me? Halley wanted to ask, wishing Jill could assist Dr. Abraham. But new nurses didn't argue with their supervisor. They followed orders.

Determined to make a better impression than she had yesterday, she strode briskly down the corridor, stopping long enough to get a bandage tray. Three-seventeen. She repeated the number to herself, going over the important facts about the case before she entered the room. Pete Mason. Age ten. Recovering from second-degree burns over twenty percent of his body. Recently transferred from the burn unit to pediatrics.

When she arrived in 317, Mark was looking at Pete's right hand and forearm. Standing a couple of feet behind him, she observed how gently Mark examined the boy. Pete's trust was obvious by the way he rested his hand on Mark's palm. Short dark hairs on

the back of his hands contrasted with the child's healing pink skin. Her eyes followed the course of the hairs
until they disappeared beneath his white cuffs.

"Nurse?"

His tone jarred Halley into action. Flustered at
being caught staring at him, anxious to please, she
shoved the tray toward him a bit too hard, nudging his
forearm. "Sorry, Doctor."

"I hope you are," he muttered under his breath as
he straightened and faced her. Halley blinked in surprise at the hushed barb. "Don't bother batting your
long lashes at me. You're wasting precious time flirting. Flirting won't hide incompetency, Nurse."

Halley ground her teeth to keep from responding.
Never had she been accused of fluttering her eyelashes or incompetency. She'd left three hospitals for
the exact reason: flirty doctors. For a second, she
wished it was his head she'd hit with the tray instead
of his arm.

"Well?" he challenged. "Are you going to stand
there until it's time to punch the time clock and go
home?"

Her violet eyes flashed as she glanced at him and
said quietly, "Doctor, I suggest you make your complaints regarding my performance to the supervising
nurse."

"That, Nurse Twain, you can count on," came his
smug reply as he selected a gauze bandage from the
tray and turned toward Pete.

Fingers trembling from the unwarranted criticism,
Halley opened the adhesive tape and moved beside
Mark. Determined not to let his comments keep her
from doing her job, she yanked a strip of tape from

the roll. She could feel Dr. Abraham's derisive gaze on her fumbling fingers as she unsuccessfully attempted to tear it.

"How long have you been a nurse?" He set the gauze back on the tray, took the tape from her hands and neatly tore off the amount he needed.

"Five years."

The disparaging look he cast her was eloquent. He might just as well have shouted, "You haven't learned much."

As he single-handedly managed to bandage Pete's arm, Halley stood beside him fuming, feeling totally useless. He politely ignored her while he bantered with Pete. Nothing, short of pushing him aside and competently applying the bandage, could redeem her self-esteem.

Pete shyly smiled at Halley. "You're as pretty as my mom."

"Pretty is as pretty does," Mark added.

"Only ugly goes through to the bone marrow, Doctor." She grinned when his supercilious smile drooped. Other nurses might worship Dr. Mark Abraham despite his caustic manner, but not her. She'd taken his insults for the last time. "Thank you, Pete." Noticing the G.I. Joe figurines on the boy's nightstand, she said, "That's a neat collection. My youngest brother..."

"All finished," Mark interrupted. Rising, he shot Halley a quieting glare and then glanced over her shoulder. "Your dad is here just in time to hear the good news. Mr. Mason, how would you like to take your son home for Thanksgiving?"

An older version of the small boy on the bed grinned from ear to ear. "That would be wonderful!"

"Do you mean it, Dr. Abraham? Can I really go home?" Pete asked excitedly. "Can I start packing?"

Mark ruffled Pete's hair. "Whoa! Thanksgiving is two days away."

Mr. Mason laughed. "He may need every minute to muster his armies."

Halley started to offer to help when she saw Mark gesture toward the door; he'd none too politely dismissed her from the room.

"See you later," she called to Pete. Open rebellion in front of a patient and his parent wasn't ethical. Sooner or later she'd have an opportunity to tell Mark Abraham exactly what she thought of his cutting remarks.

Outside the doorway, Halley inhaled deeply. Dr. Abraham was undoubtedly the rudest, most overbearing, hateful man she'd ever had the misfortune of assisting. He'd barely restrained himself from calling her incompetent, then made her too nervous even to tear a piece of adhesive tape. And last of all, he'd interfered with her establishing a rapport with his patient. She clenched her fists in anger.

"Loitering, Nurse Twain?"

"That does it!" she sputtered, ready to read him the riot act. "I don't know what your problem is, but—"

"My only problem revolves around the care of my patients," he snapped. "Pete was injured when his younger brother tossed a lit match into an empty gasoline can. His brother wasn't hurt. While Pete was in the burn unit, a psychologist spent hours working him through a mixture of anger and sibling rivalry. He didn't need to hear you running at the mouth about how terrific your brother is."

"How did you expect me to be aware of his psychological profile? For Pete's sake, Doctor, I've been on this floor for less than twenty-four hours!"

"Exactly. *For Pete's sake* I'd prefer you refrained from idle chitchat until you are familiar with a patient's medical history. Now, if you'll excuse me, I have work to do."

"You say that as though I don't," Halley blustered, impetuously blocking his departure by grabbing his arm.

A foot shorter and fifty pounds lighter than Mark, she realized how ridiculous her attempt to restrain him physically must appear. She felt his muscles tighten beneath her fingertips. His eyes dropped to her hand, then raised with scathing coolness.

"Add insensitivity to incompetence, plus the amount of time you waste, and it makes me wonder why you receive such glowing evaluations."

"I earned them!"

Mark's mouth twisted in a mockery of a smile. "I'll bet you did, Nurse Twain. I'll just bet you did. Don't expect me to give Martha Chaney rave reports because of your—"

"Hush your ugly mouth!"

Halley dropped his arm, clamping her hand over her mouth. Adding insubordination to the rest of her professional flaws increased her vulnerability. Dr. Abraham had enough influence with Nurse Chaney to force some disciplinary action if he really wanted to. She knew to avoid a stern lecture from the supervising nurse that she ought to apologize. She couldn't.

He'd unjustly provoked her. Disciplinary action be damned, she thought. He'd be a patient in the geriatric ward before she apologized! She turned on her heel, swiftly heading toward the nurses' station.

Mark watched her hasty departure. Twice she'd called him ugly. Wouldn't Cleo have loved to hear that verbal exchange? Halley and Cleo were obviously a matched pair, but Cleo was smarter. At least she had been intelligent enough to initially pretend an all-consuming passion. If this Twain woman thought she'd be able to snare a doctor by acting the way she had today, she had another think coming. But no matter what she did he wasn't going to be fooled. He'd been a willing victim of Cleo's schemes. He wouldn't make the same mistake twice. Certain her actions were just some new twist to the same old game, he promptly dismissed the possibility that Halley wasn't interested in him.

He considered recommending disciplinary action. The sooner Halley Twain was out of the pediatric ward and away from him, the better. While she'd been standing behind him, he'd actually felt her presence. It had taken all his powers of concentration to continue examining Pete. With his mind picturing her dark curly hair and violet eyes, her presence could have resulted in negligence on his part.

What had she been thinking while watching him? Ugly thoughts, he was sure. Mark glanced at his hands. Compared to the healthy pink tinge of Pete's skin, his hands were disgustingly pale. What did she expect in the middle of winter? A glowing tan?

Mark sucked in his flat stomach as he brushed his hair off his forehead.

"Primping, Dr. Abraham?" Martha teased.

"Don't be silly," Mark protested, flushing guiltily. "My patients don't notice what I look like."

"Who are you kidding? Just this morning Judy said you were the handsomest man in the world...aside from her daddy."

Uncomfortable discussing his physical appearance, Mark said, "Keep an eye on that little rascal. Last night she stashed peppermints between her sheets."

"I've scheduled Judy for another session with the dietitian. By the way, how did you and Halley get along?" Martha asked inquisitively.

Tell her, Mark goaded himself. Say it fast so you'll believe it yourself. Halley Twain is insensitive to patients, incompetent and wastes precious time.

"Reserving judgment, doctor?" Martha asked after a lengthy pause.

He lifted his shoulders in a careless shrug. "How would you react if I told you I think she's a lousy nurse?"

"I'd say you shouldn't let Jason Malone's glib stories prejudice you against her. Give Halley a chance to prove herself. Get to know her."

"No, thanks."

"Why? Afraid her charm will break through that shell you've built around yourself?"

"Don't trespass into my personal life, Nurse Chaney." Clipped tones emphasized the rebuke. "Halley Twain is just another nurse. No worse than some and no better than others."

"Then you won't object to my assigning Halley to your patients, will you?"

Mark saw the same glint in Martha's eyes that he'd seen two weeks ago. Back then, he'd made the mistake of vehemently opposing Halley's application for transfer. Objecting now would probably get the same results. "No objections."

"I thought, since she's new and eager to please, I'd ask her to help with the kids' Thanksgiving party." Martha grinned. "Oscar won't object to your including her in your ventriloquist routine, will he?"

Mark felt trapped. He'd permitted Martha to exercise her motherly instincts toward him because that helped to assure him that his patients would receive the best care available. Their age difference protected him from gossip by the hospital staff. That, in addition to his genuine fondness for Martha and his respect for her administrative capabilities, kept him from telling her to aim her Cupid's arrow in another direction. He wasn't going to be shot down again.

"Oscar would be furious."

Patting Mark on the arm, Martha nodded. "You're right."

Observing the twinkling laughter in Martha's eyes, he wondered what she meant. He didn't have to wait for her punch line.

"You're the one who said Oscar is a dummy. No red-blooded American male would ever object to Halley Twain."

Mark couldn't stop himself from grinning at the way Martha always managed to make him eat his own words. Dryly he replied, "In that case, I'd better get down to the lab immediately to have a test run on my red corpuscles."

"While you're there, have an EKG run," Martha ribbed.

"My heart is whole and sound. Precisely how I plan on keeping it."

"Well, Doctor, if your heart is in good shape, perhaps you should have a brain scan. A good nurse can always tell when something isn't working properly."

Putting his hand on her shoulder, Mark mimicked, "A good nurse can always tell when her suggestions are being politely ignored by a good doctor."

"Humph!" Martha scoffed. "I'm encouraging you to be *bad*. Have a fling! You spend so much time at St. Michael's you're beginning to smell like a hospital. Why don't you—"

"Bye, Martha."

"I'm not finished talking to you."

Mark saluted her and hightailed it toward the elevator. As he passed the nurses' station, he nodded at Tammy and scowled at Halley. She returned his dirty look, full force.

"What did you do to him?" Tammy asked Halley in a hushed voice.

"Nothing." Halley continued to make a notation on Pete's record regarding the supplies used to rebandage his arm.

"Nothing?" Tammy fanned her face. "Whew! I'm melting from the heat waves."

"You're too young for hot flashes," Halley teased, refusing to let her conflict with Dr. Abraham spoil her rapport with the remainder of the staff. "Maybe you're suffering from a vitamin deficiency."

"I'm not the only one around here who's hot under the collar. You've been pressing down so hard on that pen that the point is liable to gouge through the metal clipboard.''

Halley loosened her grip on the pen. She'd kept one eye on the conversation between Dr. Abraham and Martha Chaney while completing the routine task. Furtive glances in her direction had confirmed her suspicions. They'd been discussing her.

Martha had appeared to be doing most of the talking. The expression she'd seen on Mark's face could only be described as forbidding. Occasionally, he'd grinned, and despite her animosity, Halley had understood what Jill meant earlier about doing anything for one of his smiles. She wondered what it would take to be the recipient of his smile. The likelihood of finding out was remote.

He'd made his opinion of her perfectly clear. He thought her insensitive, incompetent, indolent. Flirty, too, she reminded herself. His unflattering opinion bothered Halley. Being new on the job was tough enough without complications.

Had he told Martha that she was incompetent? she wondered worriedly.

Halley peered down the corridor. Martha grinned at her and made a circle with her thumb and forefinger. Everything's okay, Halley interpreted, confused. Perplexed by the unexpected reaction of her immediate superior, Halley carefully returned the chart to where it belonged.

He must have kept his opinion to himself, she surmised. Why? She'd bluntly told Mark to make his complaints to Martha Chaney. Why had he waited?

Martha walked behind the counter at the nurses' station. "Any complaints about the holiday schedule, Tammy?"

"No, ma'am. Thanks for letting me have Thursday off. Thanksgiving is a big occasion for my family."

"What about you, Halley?" Martha turned, facing Halley.

"No problem with my working. My whole family is in Georgia. Fort Bragg."

"Military?"

"Yes, ma'am."

"Brothers and sisters?"

"Two of each. Holidays around my parents' house are wild with three overactive teenagers."

"Three? How old is the other one?"

Halley's eyes misted. Her sister, Katy, wouldn't be there this Thanksgiving. Strange how she still couldn't get used to thinking of holidays with only five people instead of six. "I meant two brothers and one sister."

Sensitive to the overt signs of stress, Martha moved closer to Halley. "Did you lose your sister recently?"

"Five years ago, at Christmas." The years had dulled the pain of loss, but hadn't erased it. "She was my twin."

Martha nodded, gaining insight into the error in arithmetic. Deciding to change the subject, she asked, "Would you mind helping with the special Thanksgiving party for the children?"

From her previous experience in pediatrics, as well as her experience with her sister, Halley knew how hard being in a hospital during a holiday was on children. Nurses, especially single nurses without family obligations, went all out to keep the patients from slipping into a depression that could affect their recovery. Her own problems seemed small by comparison.

"Of course I'll help." Halley knew the number of patients in the hospital would drop drastically. Doctors released their patients, if possible, before a major holiday. The incident in Pete's room was still fresh in her mind. Pete was one of the lucky ones. He'd be home for Thanksgiving. "It'll give me a chance to get to know the children better."

Tammy swiveled around in her chair. "I'll have the rest of the decorations up this afternoon. The dietitian said she'd take care of the refreshments."

"Any special entertainment planned?" Halley asked.

"Puppets by Petula. A trio of candy stripers are going to sing. The play therapist taught Judy and Sue finger-play-songs that they'll do."

Martha looked at Tammy warningly to keep the bubbly unit nurse from foiling her plans. She pulled a small pad from her skirt pocket and jotted down a phone number and address. "Dr. Oscar mentioned needing some assistance. He's the ventriloquist who regularly performs for the children's parties."

Tammy giggled, then buried her face in a stack of forms.

Accepting the slip of paper, Halley said, "I don't know a thing about ventriloquism."

"A couple of years ago, another ventriloquist had a dummy on one knee and a nurse on the other knee. It was hilarious and the kids loved it! You might suggest something like that."

"I don't know," Halley murmured, not wishing to be in the limelight. "Isn't there something behind the scenes I could do? I'm certain Jill—"

"Jill is too tall," Martha countered. "You're the right size. Of course, if you really object to helping out..."

Put like that, Halley knew any refusal would seem churlish, an unwillingness to cooperate. "No! No! I'll help however I can."

"Great! Oscar's office is in the quadrangle across from the hospital. It's such short notice, maybe you'd better contact Oscar when you take you lunch break."

"I'll take care of it," Halley replied, hearing the rattle of laden food carts as they were pushed down the hall. "I hope you won't be disappointed."

Martha grinned and poked her wire-framed glasses on her nose. "I won't be."

After a quick sandwich in his office, Mark strode into the reception area. Lu Anne, the receptionist, hadn't returned from lunch. He seated himself at her desk and glanced at the appointment book.

Alone, with only the piped-in music as a companion, he began to think of the pint-size shrew in the pediatric ward. He'd purposely tested her mettle and found her strong and resilient. Despite his accusations, she'd refused to be intimidated. Grudgingly, he had to admit he respected her spunkiness. She'd actually told him to go to Martha Chaney with his complaints.

What could he say to Martha without sounding petty? It was bad enough that Martha had caught him "primping." Martha's perceptiveness was uncanny.

Somehow, someway, she had sensed his attraction to Halley. Mark grinned wryly as he recalled her encouraging him to have a fling.

Shortly after his divorce, he'd indulged his battered ego. One-night stands were the result. But never with a nurse, *never* with a beautiful woman.

From the perspective of hindsight, Mark realized he'd sought a simple solution for a complex problem. It hadn't taken long for him to get smart, to discover that indiscriminate sex left him only with a gnawing emptiness.

Celibacy, the alternative, also had held little appeal. Doctors were human, too. Depriving himself completely of a woman's company violated one of man's basic needs.

Finally, he'd compromised. On rare occasions, he dated. If, and that was a big *if*, he and his date felt so inclined, they'd end the evening in bed.

Another simple solution for a complex problem.

Confronted with Halley Twain, he knew his days for simple solutions were drawing to a close. He could fight her tooth and nail, but he couldn't deny that he wanted her. He was fighting a losing battle with himself.

His fist slammed into his open palm as the phone rang.

"Dr. Abraham speaking."

Halley's jaw dropped. She reread the number in Martha's handwriting. "Uh, may I speak to Dr. Oscar, please."

Immediately, Mark recognized the voice on the other end of the line. He leaned back in the chair. "Who gave you this number?"

"Mrs. Chaney." The urge to babble, to fill the silence following her reply, to keep him from hanging up, made Halley doubly uncomfortable. "Is Dr. Oscar your associate?"

"In a manner of speaking." What is Martha up to now? Mark wondered. Instigating prank calls wasn't her style.

His voice lacked its usual abrasiveness when speaking to her, and Halley felt a fluttering sensation down her spine. She held the phone between her ear and shoulder as she rubbed at the goose bumps on her arms. Goose bumps? The phone slipped a notch. She fumbled, then caught it. "May I speak to him?"

Mark's finger tapped his appointment book. "He's busy with patients until after five. What do you want to talk to him about?"

Disgusted with herself for her reaction to the sound of his voice, Halley bristled. "I don't think that's any of your business, Dr. Abraham. I'll call back when Dr. Oscar is available."

"Hold the line a second." Mark put Halley on hold. Making a quick decision that he was sure he'd regret later, he punched the lit button. "Oscar is available at five-thirty. I'll book your appointment with him."

His fingers trembled as he replaced the receiver without waiting for a reply. Nervous energy drove him to his feet. He paced back and forth in the confines of the reception room until Lu Anne unlocked the outside door. Two women with small children trailed behind her.

Halley heard the line disconnect and banged down the phone. "Don't do me any favors, Dr. Abraham!" Why Dr. Oscar, a man kind enough to donate his

Thanksgiving to sick children, shared an office with Mark Abraham she'd never know.

"Something wrong?" Jill asked, entering the nurses' lounge.

"Nothing I couldn't handle with a foot-long syringe filled with tranquilizers!" Halley rose to her feet, stomping angrily toward Jill. "Who does that man think he is!"

"Who?"

Remembering Jill's comments about Mark, Halley hesitated. She wasn't going to get any sympathy from the other nurse. "Never mind. Tell me what you know about Dr. Oscar."

"Dr. Oscar? I don't think I've met him."

"You must have. He shares an office with Mark Abraham."

Jill burst into giggles. "Dr. Oscar *is* Mark Abraham."

"He can't be. He . . . Martha . . . Dr. Oscar," Halley sputtered. Her thoughts scattered. Her blood boiled. Mark was probably holding his sides with laughter, too. That was why he'd hung up so abruptly. Ten years ago, she'd have had the satisfaction of stomping her foot and bellowing in outrage. Age tempered her behavior but not her desire for satisfaction. "I must have misunderstood Martha," she said in a deceptively calm voice.

"Mark is a ventriloquist and Oscar is his dummy. Martha says Oscar is Mark's alter ego. As sexy as that little fellow is, I'd say he's Mark's libido."

Jill opened her lunch bag and pulled out two hard-boiled eggs. From the grim look on her face, Halley knew Jill wished those eggs had hatched and grown into a king-sized chicken salad sandwich.

"I'll keep that in mind when I meet Oscar this afternoon. Thanks for saving me from looking like a nincompoop."

Breaking the shell of the egg by tapping it on the table, Jill eyed Halley carefully. "Wonder why Mark didn't straighten you out about his alias."

"Who knows? I've been near the man twice and each time he acts like he'd like to bite my head off."

"Oh, yeah? That doesn't sound like Mark—or Oscar." She peeled off the shell, laughing huskily. Her blue eyes glazed dreamily. "Sounds like someone familiar, though. I know what I'd do if I had him alone, in his office, without any interruptions."

Halley groaned. "Eat your egg and spare me the details, would you?"

"And repress my fantasies? Um-umm! Repressed fantasies make a person crazy. First, I'd lace my fingers behind his neck." She chuckled. "Don't want to take any chances on his getting away. Then, I'd kiss that little dimple in his right cheek. Next, I'd circle the lobe of his ear with my fingernail. That drives a man wild. I wouldn't rush anything. Ever so slowly, I'd..."

"You'll have to excuse me," Halley said, opening the door to hide her flaming pink face. Jill's monologue brought vivid pictures to Halley's mind. The only difference between what Jill said and what Halley saw was whose lips and hands were doing the touching and kissing. "I'm late."

"Halley?" Jill said after taking a bite of her egg. "Do you consider yourself worldly?"

"Nurses are born worldly," Halley quipped.

"When I was a kid in practice nursing, I used to think worldliness was determined by how many naked male bodies a woman had seen. That would make nurses far more worldly than other women. Do you think there's a direct correlation between naked bodies and worldliness?"

"Something tells me this is a rhetorical question," Halley muttered. "You don't really expect an answer, do you?"

Jill swallowed, then grinned. "In a roundabout way, I was going to ask you if you'd made it this far in nursing without seeing any naked men. Something tells me that you're almost as naive as you look."

"I'm not naive." Jason had destroyed her naïveté. "Gullible, maybe. Naive? No."

"Really?" Jill looked deeply into Halley's eyes, as if she could discern the truth there.

"Really." Halley seldom varnished the truth to make herself look good. From the rubble of her relationship with Jason, she'd learned a few positive lessons. Telling lies caused problems; it didn't solve them. "I may look young on the outside, but on the inside I'm wrinkled with age. Worldly."

"I like you, Halley. That says a lot for you. I usually shy away from attractive women."

Those were the first kind words Halley had heard in weeks that weren't based in sympathy. In essence, Jill was offering her friendship. To allay any misconceptions, Halley said, "My meeting with Oscar is strictly business. Martha asked me to assist him at the party."

Suddenly Halley lurched forward when she felt two hands circle her waist.

"What have we here?" a smooth voice asked from too close to Halley's ear.

"Dr. Daniel Edwards, meet Halley Twain, recently transferred to pediatrics from ER," Jill introduced.

Halley turned, freeing herself from the man's grasp. She saw the way his blue eyes widened with interest as he leisurely examined her from her dark hair to her size-five shoes. "I'm glad to meet you," Halley said, politely offering her hand.

"And I'm glad to meet you." He took her hand with both of his. "I can't believe you've been working at St. Michael's and we've never met. I make a point of meeting all the beautiful women."

"Translated that's the same as the trite 'Where have you been all my life?'" Jill said dryly. Then, giving Dr. Edwards a devilish grin, she asked, "What's up, Doc?"

"Nothing you'd be interested in," he suavely replied. "Halley, would you like a cup of coffee?"

He was still holding her hand, and Halley wondered how she could escape without appearing rude. His blond hair, blue eyes and classical good looks matched Jill's. He looked as if he spent a good deal of time in expensive gyms, and he reeked of woodsy cologne and breath mints. Only a small piece of adhesive tape across the bridge of his nose marred his perfection.

Withdrawing her fingers, she excused herself. "I'm late."

"Those two words are at the top of Daniel's hate list," Jill joked. "By the way, Doc, how's your nose?"

Hostility palpitated between Daniel and Jill. Be it love or hate, Halley wasn't going to enter the fracas!

"Healing, no thanks to you," he replied, his eyes remaining on Halley. "How about a drink after work?"

"Sorry. I have an appointment."

"With Dr. Abraham," Jill added, taking another bite of her egg. "Did Tony Miller get more of your time than it took to boil this egg?"

Daniel shot Jill a withering glance. Smile back in place, he dropped the pitch of his voice to a husky level. "Tomorrow night? Dinner?"

Halley shook her head. She hated men that moved too fast.

"Saturday? I'll have to break a date, but for you..."

"Cripes, Daniel. Your nose hasn't even healed yet!"

Halley dodged around Daniel Edwards. "Thanks, but no thanks."

Tight-lipped, Halley left the lounge. Daniel Edwards was a bit older, and a bit smoother than Jason, but they were cut from the same cloth. Like Jill, Halley didn't want any part of Dr. Edwards's games. At the moment, there was only one man she could think of whose games she liked less: Mark Abraham.

Chapter Three

Halley tried to corner Martha before the end of her shift, but failed. The woman was as elusive as a ghost. One minute Halley would see her entering a room, the next, she'd be gone. Halley found herself muttering to empty walls.

Two related thoughts worried her. One, why had Martha led her to believe Dr. Oscar would be the person Halley was to assist at the party? And two, why had Mark gone along with the deception? Were they playing some kind of bizarre joke on her?

Those worrisome thoughts eventually produced others. Did her supervising nurse know about the conflict between Halley and Martha's favorite doctor? If so, why was she pushing them together?

Being forced into the company of someone she disliked reminded Halley of her mother's favorite punishment. When she and her brothers and sisters wanted to argue, her mother would isolate them in a room and make them work together. Was Martha using the same technique? Did she believe mere proximity would diminish Mark's animosity?

Halley doubted it would work. For some unfathomable reason, Mark disliked her intensely. If Halley had believed in reincarnation, she'd have sworn that in a previous life Mark must have been Wild Bill Hickock and she'd been Annie Oakley—natural enemies despite their attraction to each other.

Jason had frequently praised Mark's ability. Nurses throughout the hospital acted as if he walked on water. Pete trusted him. Despite her own feelings she couldn't ignore everyone's opinion of Mark. After all, a man who cared for sick children couldn't be all bad. Besides, children were good judges of character, and they seemed to like him. Dr. Mark Abraham must be a man worthy of admiration.

Admiration, she mused, differentiating how the children felt from her own intense feelings. She cautioned herself about confusing love with admiration. That shouldn't be too difficult considering Mark's hostility. Despite Martha's good intentions, the last place Halley imagined Mark Abraham would want to be was in a locked room with her.

Then why didn't he say, "I'm Oscar. I don't need your assistance"? In Pete's room, he hadn't had any qualms about blasting her.

Was he hiding behind a dummy?

You're the dummy, Halley silently chastised herself as she walked down the corridor toward the elevator. You should be concentrating on establishing a low profile, one of an efficient and silent nurse. But instead you're walking into the limelight when you should be hiding!

Her five-thirty appointment with Dr. Oscar had given her the excuse she'd needed to spend additional time acquainting herself with the nurses on the three-to-eleven shift. Since Mark realized her shift was over at three o'clock, he must have decided she needed the extra hours to make up for any time she'd wasted. That thought generated enough heat to take the chill off the winter air as Halley, following Jill's directions, crossed the quadrangle to the doctors' private offices.

Halley opened the door to Mark's waiting room. It was deserted. She glanced through the sliding glass windows above the receptionist's desk. Empty.

The man really had his nerve. He'd booked her an appointment with the fictitious Dr. Oscar, then canceled without notifying her. "Dr. Abraham?" she called.

Her violet eyes glanced around the waiting room anxiously. He must be a Garfield fan, she mused, noticing the walls covered with fat, tiger-striped cats. Colorful geometric mobiles hung from the fluorescent light fixtures. One secluded area was set up with child-size tables and chairs. Puzzles and popular toys were neatly placed on bookshelves lining the walls. She noticed a computer and videocassettes in the opposite corner.

Something for everyone, she thought. *Except me.*

"Dr. Abraham?" She waited a moment then raised her voice again and called, "Mark?"

A scraping noise coming from behind Halley startled her.

"Hi, Cutie-pie! Take your coat off and stay awhile."

The receptionist's window was open. Sitting on the ledge, swinging his legs, was a dapper ventriloquist's dummy dressed in a miniature version of a doctor's scrub suit. Reddish brown hair matched the freckles liberally sprinkled across his nose. Large, expressive brown eyes seemed to watch her remove her coat and drape it over the back of a chair. They followed her every step toward the window as though they could see. Both lids drooped lazily. "What's wrong, beautiful? Cat got your tongue?"

Mad as she'd been when Jill had told her who Dr. Oscar really was, Halley couldn't help but smile at the dummy.

"Dr. Oscar, I presume?"

The dummy squirmed, bobbing his head up and down. "Nurse Twain, I presume?" Oscar mimicked. "You call me Oscar; I'll call you Snookums."

"Where's Dr. Abraham?" The dummy's features were so lifelike, so animated, she almost felt as if she were talking to a real person.

"Whooo-hooo! Mark! Come out, come out, wherever you are." Oscar leaned forward, scanning the room. His lashes fluttered. "The old workaholic must have cut out early. You know what they say about workaholic doctors, don't you?"

Halley shook her head. Playing the straight man for his joke, she asked, "What do they say about workaholic doctors?"

"Old doctors never die, they just smell that way."
Oscar slapped his knees at his own joke and hee-
hawed.

"Is that your official medical opinion?" Halley
asked, playing along.

"Hmmm." His neck stretched upward as he cleared
his throat. "Hmm."

Halley chuckled. She'd heard dozens of doctors
make the same profound sound. Fascinated by the way
Oscar's mouth moved with each syllable, she reached
toward the dummy's face.

"Wanna touch me, don't you?" His lids lowered
slightly, but his eyes followed her hand. His voice
dropped to a gravelly, come-hither pitch. "Do I get to
touch you? Fair's fair."

His small gloved hand reached forward, much lower
than Halley's face.

"You lech!" Halley said, slapping Oscar's hand
playfully. "Ever had your face slapped, my pint-size
friend?" Halley's rebuke was softened by a grin.

"Never! Haven't you heard? I'm the nurses' favorite doctor!" His eyes opened wide. "Whaddaya mean
by pint-size? Was that a short-people joke?" Oscar
demanded. "I hate short-people jokes! You aren't exactly Wilt Chamberlain yourself."

"Sorry. I didn't know you were sensitive about your
size."

Halley couldn't believe she'd just apologized to a
carved block of wood. Rising on tiptoe, she tried to
lean past Oscar to find Mark.

"Aaa-aaa-aaa!" Oscar swayed to one side, blocking her vision. "Your apology doesn't suffice. We've

had our first official fight. Now, we have to make up properly.''

"How?''

''If you're really, *really* sorry, I'll let you kiss my cheek. Once. But you have to promise not to get carried away. After all, we are in Dr. Workaholic's office.'' Oscar tipped forward. As though he was about to tell a state secret, he whispered, ''The doc is jealous of my good looks. All the nurses want to take my clothes off and look at my bod.''

''I'll try to control myself,'' Halley promised, her amethyst eyes twinkling with mirth.

Suddenly the dummy's voice became Mark's. ''We both know how ugly Dr. Abraham is.''

Apologize now, Halley's conscience demanded. Mark wasn't ugly to the bone nor was his mouth ugly. Quite the contrary.

''I'm sorry about that, too.''

Oscar grinned, then his head spun in a complete circle. ''Wow! Another apology! You gonna kiss Dr. Ugly Workaholic, too?''

''Can't.'' Two could play Mark's hiding game. ''He isn't here.''

''Close your eyes and pucker up, Snookums! I think I hear his footsteps.''

Oscar disappeared. In his place, stood Mark, scowling.

''Oscar is darling,'' Halley mumbled inanely, feeling extremely ridiculous. ''Clever.''

''He's a dummy.''

Halley bristled. She'd disguised her compliment by using Oscar's name. For a man reputed to be extremely intelligent, he certainly acted obtuse.

"He's smarter than some blockheads I know," she huffed indignantly.

Was that a muscle in Mark's cheek flexing in anger, or was he about to laugh? The corners of his mouth barely lifted in answer to Halley's silent query. Oscar's outrageous behavior had changed her scowls into smiles. Maybe Mark needed some of the same treatment.

"I wonder which of you is the best kisser?"

It was Mark's turn to feel his face flame. With Oscar as his spokesman, he could say and do anything. Without the dummy, Mark's insecurities surfaced. "I haven't kissed Oscar. How should I know?"

Her eyes lit up with amusement. Was Mark Abraham, doctor extraordinaire, bashful?

"Get Oscar up here and we'll conduct a kissing test." She imitated Oscar's flirty wink.

"You can't kiss Oscar. Lipstick ruins his paint job."

Halley inched forward, peering over the counter into the receptionist's office. Oscar lay on the desk, as though sleeping.

"Another one of life's little disappointments. I seem to have a knack for choosing the wrong men." Realizing she'd said far more than she'd intended, she backed away from the sliding glass. Blindly, she reached for her coat. "I don't think I can add anything to Oscar's performance at the Thanksgiving party. You're far more clever than I am."

"Running, Snookums?" Halley heard Oscar ask when she reached the door. Turning, she saw the dummy was once again in Mark's arms. "Here I got her all puckered and ready, and what do you do? You blow it! You dummy!" Oscar ranted, glaring at Mark.

Halley watched Mark's mouth for movement, but his lips remained still.

"Stop calling me a dummy," Mark protested.

"Okay, Dr. Ugly Workaholic. I won't call you a dummy." Oscar winked at Halley. "We'll have to keep his being an uncouth dummy as a little secret between you and me."

Mark groaned. "Don't talk to Snookums as though I've left the room. I can hear everything you're saying."

"What do you think you are, Doc? Some sort of a mind reader?" Oscar's neck twisted until he faced the back wall. "I don't see any degrees in psychology hanging back here."

"Don't be ridiculous, Oscar! I know exactly what you're thinking before you say it."

Halley drew closer, mesmerized. "How do you do that?"

"What? Make him talk?" Oscar asked. Mark's face assumed a totally blank expression. "I stick my hand under his clothes and he responds. Wanna try?"

"You're awful." Halley giggled.

"Hear that, dummy? She thinks you're awful. A chip off the old block." Oscar tossed back his head and laughed. "I can make the doc do anything."

"Make him smile."

One side of Mark's lips curved into a lopsided grin.

"Bigger," Halley cued.

Slowly, the other side lifted.

"Teeth. Give me a big, toothy smile," Halley said, as if trying to increase the level of Mark's performance beyond Oscar's ability. "Can you make him laugh?"

"Lordy, lordy, Snookums. You're asking a lot. Let me see. There has to be a funny button in here somewhere." Oscar bent at the waist and nuzzled Mark's neck. "I . . . can't . . . seem . . . to . . . find . . . it."

"Try around his ribs," Halley suggested.

Seconds later, after thoroughly mussing the front of Mark's shirt, Oscar's little shoulders hunched with dejection. His mouth drooped. "Aw darn, I can't find it anywhere. The brochure said this model comes fully equipped. I paid for a funny button and didn't get one. What's America coming to when it puts out a poor specimen like this? Do you think I ought to send him back to the manufacturer?"

"Maybe." Halley pretended to ponder the dilemma. "Did you get a money-back guarantee?"

Shaking his head, Oscar replied, "Naw. You only get those with the expensive models. Mark's from the economy line, but he's supposed to be able to do everything the deluxe model can do. Why, he's even guaranteed not to smear his paint job when kissed."

Mark's smile became decidedly wicked. Without a forbidding scowl marring his face, Halley saw that he was devastatingly handsome. She saw something else, too. Longing? Yearning? Quickly, she looked away from him. Her own loneliness must have made her imagine it.

Halley seriously considered taking Oscar up on his blatant attempt to coax her into kissing Mark. "Lipstick proof, huh?"

"Yeah, but who'd want to kiss him? He's such an ugly old toad." Oscar shrugged, batting his eyelashes. "You're a nurse. Do you think you could locate his funny button?"

"I doubt it," Halley replied honestly. She knew precisely where his scowl button was, though. Right in the center of her forehead. All he had to do to punch his button was look at her.

"You aren't being much help, Snookums," Oscar complained. "I thought nurses were angels of mercy and were able to do anything."

"Nurses aren't miracle workers," she countered, giving Mark a dirty look. His toothy grin remained steadfast.

Halley watched Oscar's head raise as though he'd been struck with a brilliant idea.

"I've got it! Do you remember the story about the princess and the frog?"

"Yes," Halley said cautiously.

"Why don't you take this old toad home with you, put him on your pillow, kiss him, and we'll see if he turns into a prince!"

Laughing at the preposterous idea, Halley declined by shaking her head.

"Think of the money you'd save me on parts and labor." Oscar bounced up and down. "I think it's your duty as a professional nurse."

Halley lifted her eyes toward Mark. "What do you think, Mark?"

"I want you." His voice held a robotlike quality.

"Stop playing games." Halley stepped sideways until she was standing in the doorway of the receptionist's room. She watched Mark put Oscar in a velvet-lined trunk. "Let's get serious."

Mark straightened, his scowl firmly affixed once more. His dark eyes seemed to bore into hers. Oscar's tenor voice replied, "Let's get physical."

Flustered, she felt her heart pound furiously. Oscar is Mark, Mark is Oscar, she reminded herself. They are one and the same.

Reality seemed strangely out of focus. Time stood still. Her breath caught in her throat when Mark opened his arms. There was something so vulnerable, so touching in the simple gesture that she couldn't refuse. Mindlessly, like a homing pigeon, she walked into his welcoming arms.

Mark hugged her tightly. She fit perfectly. His long, lonely emptiness was filled with her softness. His chin nuzzled gently against her dark curls.

Halley rubbed against his chest, not certain that what was taking place was for real. The masculine fragrance teasing her nose smelled real. Her hands roamed over his well-muscled back. He felt real. Her eyelashes fluttered against his shirt. She wasn't having one of Jill's fanciful dreams. Mark was holding her as though he'd never let her go.

Slowly, she raised her head as he lowered his.

His eyes communicated, *I'm not sure about this.*

Hers replied, *I'm not either.*

Their closed lips brushed lightly, tentatively, uncertainly.

"Halley," Mark breathed her name, his deeply rooted protective instincts momentarily taking control. "I hate how you make me feel."

"I promised myself I'd never let another doctor take advantage of me," she whispered, feeling her breasts press against his hard chest as his arms tightened around her.

"I've been married . . . and dumped."

Halley nibbled his lower lip. "I've been dumped...without marriage."

"You're beautiful. Beautiful and desirable. I hate beautiful women."

"I hate doctors who talk when there are better things to do."

"I want more than hand holding and kissing."

"Wanting isn't enough. I've been *wanted*."

"Love? Is that what you want?"

"The impossible dream."

"Dreams die young."

"Dreams can heal."

"Or destroy."

"Then let go of me before we're both destroyed." The tip of her tongue traced his bottom lip. "Let go. I'll leave."

"I wish I could."

His lips covered hers, silencing her as he'd wanted to from the first time he'd seen her in the elevator. His tongue pushed into the honeyed moistness of her mouth. Her taste exploded over him. She was sweet, deliciously passionate, his starved senses registered, delving deeper. He caught the low, sexy moan that came from the back of her throat. He shuddered, feeling his blood heating, thawing his heart as it pounded in his ears.

Reciprocating fully, Halley swayed against him. He stole her breath, then miraculously replaced it. Her breasts hardened, tips tingling. Her knees threatened to buckle. Her feet parted, as he wedged his foot between hers, his thigh between hers. She surrendered to his strength. A heavy, achy sensation centered itself low in the pit of her stomach.

With a demanding urgency, Mark's hands skimmed her shoulders, her waist. He ground her hips against his. Her thighs clamped against his. She'd trapped him. Trapped him.

He pushed her away as though scalded by her heat. Pivoting on the ball of his foot, he turned his back on her. Pain squeezed a knot in his gut.

"You'd better go, Halley." His words were sharp, punctuated with small gasps as he tried to get his breathing under control.

Bewildered, stunned by his abruptness, Halley stumbled backward until the back of her legs touched the desk. "What happened?"

"Nothing," he blurted.

"Not from where I'm standing." She grabbed his arm. Anger gave her the strength to whip him around. Her palm itched to wipe the scowl from his face. "Was this another one of your little tests? I failed the one in the elevator...and the one in the pediatric ward. Were you testing me to see if Oscar's charm could get me into your bed!"

"You said you'd leave if I told you to go. I'm telling you. Go!" His fingers bit into her arms. "We'll both be better off."

Halley dug her heels into the carpet, resisting the pull of his hands. Realization of what had happened struck her. She'd seen too much, gotten too close. His hands trembled, a dead giveaway of his inner turmoil.

"You're scared, aren't you?" she demanded as he hustled her toward the door. "What are you afraid of?"

He forced himself to let his hands drop before he pulled her back into his arms and finished what they'd started. He had to drive her away permanently.

"Like your past supervisor, you're overrating yourself," he snarled. "Jason Malone gave you top scores, too. In fact he couldn't keep his mind on his job because all he could think about was you."

Halley blanched. "That's a slanderous lie."

"The truth isn't slander. Can't you face the truth?"

"The truth?" Halley laughed harshly. "You don't know anything about my relationship with Jason."

"Don't let Oscar's jokes fool you. I have eyes and ears. I saw Jason drag himself to work every day. Two hours after he arrived, he was a limp dishrag. Do you want to know what I heard him say?"

Halley covered her ears to avoid hearing Mark repeat Jason's recriminations as though they were the truth. Jason was a seasoned liar. She knew she wasn't the reason behind his arriving at the hospital exhausted. In fact, she'd ranted and raved at Jason for staying out until all hours of the morning when he should have been sleeping. Bleary-eyed, often drunk, he'd bellow, "Why aren't you woman enough to keep me here? It's your fault. Your sexy body promises a spectacular show, but you're like your namesake. Halley's Comet! Ha! You're a dud. You fizzle out between the sheets."

He had steadfastly followed the same pattern of behavior: recrimination followed by abject apologies.

He'd cry, begging her to love him, to stay with him. He'd said he needed her, that he couldn't survive without her. He'd blamed his drinking on stress, saying he needed to unwind from the grim realities of sickness and death.

Jason had milked her compassionate nature until she was bone-dry. Finally, after hearing the same blustering, the same weak excuses, over and over again, she'd become deaf to his emotional blackmail. She'd packed her bags. Only Jason's threat of dropping out of his internship program kept them living together, but separately. She staunchly refused to share his bed.

Finally, he'd left. Rumors circulated among the staff: Jason Malone had deserted Halley Twain. How far the rumors were from fact. His leaving was cause for celebration, not tears. Her compassionate nature, the quality that made her a fine nurse, had made her a sucker for a weak and manipulative man. Her desire to nurture and heal, attitudes suited for the children's ward, made her an easy target for a man who wanted to take without giving. Her virtues had led her to humiliation.

Mark clamped his fingers around Halley's slender wrists. "You're going to listen!"

"No!" Halley jerked her wrists loose. Her chest heaved. "Don't repeat Jason's lies. I've heard them. I'll tell you what he *should* have said. 'Doctors use nurses. They find weaknesses and exploit them.' Is that what happened in your marriage, Doc? Did you take everything offered, then callously divorce your wife?"

Gritting his teeth to bear the pain, Mark shouted, "Get out, Halley, while you can."

Pride saved Halley. Mark wasn't interested in hearing the truth. He'd made his diagnosis: she had almost ruined Jason's medical career. Lifting her chin, she picked up her coat and flung it across her shoulders. Wordlessly, back straight, she turned and walked to the door. Her legs were rubbery, barely supporting her weight, but she made it to the door.

Tears blurred her vision. She blinked and pushed the door open, letting the cold air envelop her. Halfway across the courtyard she realized her coat was unbuttoned. Automatically, she clamped the lapels under her chin. Buttoning the coat wouldn't remove the coldness surrounding her heart.

Forget his kisses, she silently chided. He was testing you. From one encounter he realized Jason was right. You aren't worth the effort. You're a well-packaged dud.

At least she hadn't made the mistake of falling in love with him. Or had she?

Long before Jason left, the mild passion he stirred in her had dwindled into nothingness. She'd assumed he'd killed her physical cravings for affections. Mark had reawakened those feelings. His kiss had been like an unexpected explosion. Balls of fire had rocketed through her. Passion flared with burning intensity. She could still feel the hot imprint of his hands. His withdrawal left her hungering for more.

Halley shivered. She couldn't let Mark destroy her. She had to get tough.

"Jason said you're one tough cookie," she muttered to remind herself. "Tough cookies don't crumble." A bitter laugh burst from her throat. "Jason probably lied about that, too."

Chapter Four

Something's wrong with my son." Mrs. Miller, Tony's mother, stood directly in front of Halley with her hand on her hips. "You're new here, aren't you?"

"Yes, ma'am," Halley replied.

"When is Dr. Edwards going to be here?"

"He'll make his evening rounds between five and six, after office hours. Can I give him a message or have Dr. Edwards call you?"

Mrs. Miller curtly nodded and turned toward Tony's room. Pausing, she wheeled around. "Have you noticed anything...unusual in Tony's behavior?"

"He's quiet."

"Too quiet. He's hatching up something," Mrs. Miller added. "And it's always something wild. Why can't he accept his limitations?"

Halley knew her limitations. Dr. Edwards was the one who should be having this conversation with Tony's mother. She'd checked Tony's medical history. Since the Miller family had moved into the area two years ago from out of state, only Tony had received counseling. And that had been sporadic.

Lately, Tony's behavior had undergone a radical transformation. No complaints. No rebellion. He passively resisted treatment by being uncommunicative.

Unable to ignore Mrs. Miller's appeal for help, Halley said, "His energy needs to be channeled—"

"*Channeled?* Raging rivers can be channeled, but not my son's energy." Mrs. Miller gave a weary sigh. "He blames me. He hurts himself to get even with me."

Halley signaled to Tammy that she'd be leaving the nursing station. "Mrs. Miller, why don't we go to the family lounge and talk?"

On the way down the corridor, Halley noticed Mark in Judy's room. He held an orange in one hand and a hypodermic needle in the other. From the pout on Judy's face, Halley could tell she wasn't hearing anything that pleased her. But at least Mark took time with his patients. He cared.

Dr. Edwards had a glib tongue with his patients, as well as the nursing staff, but Halley saw through his phony bedside manner. If a patient needed more than three minutes of his precious time, too bad. Daniel had other patients to tend, other nurses to tease, other enjoyable pursuits such as golf, tennis and swimming. To Daniel, practicing medicine was little more

than a lucrative career. To Mark, medicine was his life.
The difference between the two doctors was glaring.

Halley seated herself next to Mrs. Miller on a sofa.

"Why do you think Tony is trying to get even with
you?" Halley asked.

"It's obvious. He knows hemophilia is genetically
passed from mother to son. At best, Tony tolerates
me. At worst, he hates me for mollycoddling him.
That's what he calls it."

"What do you call it?"

"Love."

Halley observed Mrs. Miller nervously pressing the
pleats in the front of her skirt, waiting, listening.

"I *do* love him." One hand fluttered, covering her
mouth. "Sometimes loving isn't easy."

From Mrs. Miller's body language, Halley realized
that she'd admitted something she seldom expressed,
perhaps something she was ashamed of.

"Loving isn't always easy," Halley agreed. "How
do you feel when Tony is being difficult?"

"Angry."

"Do you think other parents feel angry with their
children?"

"Of course. But their children aren't hospitalized if
they're spanked."

"Has Tony been hospitalized because you spanked
him?"

"Never! I wouldn't spank him."

"You're a good mother," Halley said soothingly.
From the surprised reaction her statement brought,
Halley knew Mrs. Miller had received little praise.
"All mothers get angry at their kids. That's okay, isn't
it?"

Mrs. Miller's chin dropped, then she shook her head back and forth.

"Let's talk about your anger. When do you get angry at Tony?"

"When he does something that scares me. He knows he can't play football, or soccer, or ice hockey. I scream and yell at him, but he does it anyway."

"How do you feel when Tony is injured?" Halley knew they were finally getting to the source of Mrs. Miller's problem. Tony's mother fidgeted with her watch, the cuff of her blouse, then her wedding ring. Halley reached over and placed a comforting hand on Mrs. Miller. "Tell me."

"Guilty as all hell. It's my fault he's sick."

"So, you feel angry, and scared, and guilty. That's a heavy burden for a mother. Have you talked to your husband about the way you feel? Tony is his child, too."

"Bill doesn't say much."

From her reply, Halley gathered that Tony's parents didn't express their frustrations. Many parents of chronically ill patients had difficulty communicating their fears and anxieties. They isolated themselves from each other.

Halley remembered her own parents' closeness because of her twin sister's illness. At eight, Katy had been diagnosed as having cystic fibrosis. During the next ten years, Halley's parents had helped each other go through parental denial, avoidance and anger. And they'd helped Halley and her younger brother and sister understand their own mixed emotions. With the guidance of the doctors, nurses and family counselors, they'd coped. They'd felt joy with each remission and sorrow at the final outcome. But always, they'd shared the highs and the lows.

"Does he avoid Tony?" Halley asked thoughtfully.

"He loves Tony, too." Mrs. Miller glanced from one corner of the room to the other. Maintaining eye contact with her was impossible. "I know he does."

From the corner of her eyes, Halley saw Mark enter the lounge and quietly seat himself in the chair farthest away from them. Her stomach twisted. Mark didn't trust her competency. He probably thought she was goofing off, loafing. Even though Daniel Edwards was the doctor of record, Mark must have felt responsible to make certain she didn't harm the patient by talking to Tony's mother.

"I'm certain he does," Halley said as reassuringly as she could.

"When Tony was a little boy, I used to get so mad when Bill brought home toys that Tony could get hurt playing with. Bill gave presents, and I'd have to take them away and hide them. Then Tony would scream and yell. 'Mean old mom' is Tony's favorite description of me."

"Did you feel mean?"

"Yeah. I felt mean for protecting Tony from his father's good intentions. Bill and I went round and round. Now, Bill doesn't bring anything home. I feel guilty about that, too." Mrs. Miller sighed over her no-win situation. "Mean old mom."

Mark sank deeper into his chair as he watch Halley alternately question and reassure Mrs. Miller. What made Mrs. Miller open up to Halley? he wondered. Several nurses had approached Tony's mother, but she'd distrusted them. Halley appeared to do more listening than talking. Was that her secret? Occasionally, she'd ask a question or make a suggestion.

His respect for Halley grew with each passing minute. Although he was certain she had a multitude of tasks to perform, she appeared unhurried and calm. She'd be working late again tonight.

That won't last long, he told himself sadly. Party girls can change to make a good impression, but the change was always temporary. Give her a week, two at the most, and she'd be stir-crazy. She must be sticking close to the hospital to find a replacement for Jason, he reasoned.

He wondered who her next victim would be. She'd almost ensnared him, but he'd been smart enough and lucky enough to evade her tactics. Why didn't he feel smart or lucky? he wondered. Instead he felt like a dummy.

Mark avoided delving too deeply into his mixed feelings about Halley. What he saw and heard conflicted sharply with everything Jason had told him. Halley had refused to defend herself. She could have. She must have known in the heat of passion that he wanted to believe her.

Time and again during the night, he'd wondered what would have happened if he hadn't come to his senses and pushed her away. One thing was for certain, he would have gotten a good night's rest instead of practically strangling himself in his bed sheets.

Through Oscar, Mark had ridiculed himself for being the world's biggest blockhead. Mark recognized the role Oscar played in his life: through Oscar, Mark was able to voice his repressed emotions.

As far back as he could remember, his family had had an Oscar. In his childhood, his mother would say, "There must be an Oscar around here doing bad things. None of you kids admit to anything." While other families had mischievous ghosts or phantoms wreaking havoc on their household, the Abrahams had Oscar. Poor Oscar was blamed for eating in the parlor and getting food on the carpet. A mysteriously broken window was blamed on Oscar. Anything missing or broken was blamed on Oscar.

Mark remembered getting his first ventriloquist's doll when he was ten. The entire family chose Oscar to be the dummy's name. When Mark learned to disguise his voice and started making snappy remarks, everyone listened and laughed. Up until Oscar's arrival, as a middle child in a boisterous family, he'd been lost in the shuffle. He'd been a quiet, solitary, inhibited child. With his parents' encouragement and his siblings' laughter, Mark developed a personality for Oscar that was totally outrageous. Through Oscar, Mark had gained family recognition and love.

Mark's attention was drawn back to Mrs. Miller when she rose to her feet and hugged Halley. He rose, also.

"Aren't you Dr. Abraham?" Mrs. Miller inquired.

Halley, realizing she should have introduced Mark, quickly rectified her lapse in manners.

"Mrs. Miller, Dr. Abraham," she said, keeping her eyes on Tony's mother.

"You're the doctor who occasionally brings a ventriloquist's doll into the ward, aren't you?"

Mark nodded.

"Tony literally begged for one."

While Mark and Mrs. Miller exchanged pleasantries, Halley mulled over the idea of asking Mark to teach Tony how to manipulate a dummy. Tony couldn't hurt himself. For once, safety wasn't a problem. Perhaps Tony could vent some of his hostility in a constructive manner.

"Oscar is performing at the Thanksgiving party. Maybe Tony could be part of the act," Halley suggested with enthusiasm.

Mrs. Miller beamed. "Would you mind, Dr. Abraham? I think part of the reason behind Tony's silent treatment is that he's bored."

"Thanksgiving is the day after tomorrow," Mark said thoughtfully. "That isn't much time."

Halley watched Tony's mother's smile disappear. Glaring at Mark, she frantically searched her mind for some gimmick to pull Tony out of his despondency.

Before Halley could open his mouth, Mark said, "Don't worry, I'll think of something. Of course, I'd prefer as a professional courtesy that Dr. Edwards be informed."

"You won't be . . . uh, stepping on his medical toes so to speak, by helping with Tony, will you?" Mrs. Miller asked.

"This is a special occasion. I'm certain Dr. Edwards won't object to anything that will help Tony." Halley said it, but wasn't certain she believed it. Mark was ominously quiet. Dr. Edwards could very well object to having another doctor work with his patient.

"If he does, I'll speak to the play therapist about Tony," Mark said.

"Thank you. Both of you." Mrs. Miller glanced at her watch. "Do you mind if I mention this to Tony before I leave? He'll be thrilled."

"Why don't we wait until morning?" Mark suggested. "If Dr. Edwards doesn't object, I'll bring Oscar with me on my morning rounds."

Mrs. Miller nodded, smiled, thanked them again and briskly strode toward her son's room.

"Why do you have to have Dr. Edwards's permission? You aren't treating Tony for his illness. You aren't taking a penny of the medical fee, are you?" Halley demanded, disappointed that Tony wouldn't get the good news immediately.

"Protocol, to answer your first question. And no, I'm not going to bill the Millers for the pleasure of teaching Tony the rudiments of ventriloquism."

"You're afraid Edwards will think you're stealing his patient, aren't you?"

"Not afraid, cautious," Mark corrected.

"The sacred brotherhood of doctors. Humph! Do you realize that in the past two days, your *brother* has spent exactly twelve . . ."

"I don't want to hear what Dr. Edwards has or has not done."

"You'll listen to another doctor's lies, but not to the truth coming from a nurse?" Halley scoffed.

Mark felt the sparks of electricity shooting from her violet eyes. What could he say? At the time, he'd believed Jason. Now, he wasn't so sure.

"Let's agree to disagree on anything Jason Malone said."

Halley turned to leave. "Whatever you say, Doctor. You'll have to excuse me. Breathing the rarefied air surrounding you is making me dizzy."

"Breathing your perfume makes me a little dizzy myself." The pitch of his voice was somewhere between Oscar's and his own. She turned her head in time to see the corners of his mouth lift. "I'll help with Dr. Edwards and Tony in any way that I can."

Her smile expressed her gratitude.

"Halley?"

The sound of his voice saying her name sent a shiver down her spine. "Yes?"

Mark wanted to praise her for the compassion she'd shown Mrs. Miller. He wanted to let her know he'd spent the night thinking about her. But just as he was about to tell her, his courage failed him. "Nothing. I'll speak to Edwards."

Later that afternoon, while Halley was taping her notes for the nurse coming on duty, she saw Dr. Edwards hustling into Tony's room. Within five minutes, he was breathing down her back.

"Could I speak to you in private for a moment, please?"

His manners were impeccable, but his pale eyes liberally roamed over her.

"Yes, sir," Halley replied in as businesslike a tone as she could manage. She turned off the tape recorder and waited for him to precede her into the conference room.

Smiling, he bowed slightly, swinging his arm toward the office.

The outdated, courtly gesture displeased Halley. She wished Jill were around to cut him down to size. He still had the tape on the bridge of his nose, she noticed.

"Mark mentioned Mrs. Miller's idea of having Tony play with a ventriloquist's dummy with your supervision. Tony appears to be adjusting to hospital routine. He's improving daily."

"He's withdrawn."

Daniel chuckled. "Thank heavens for small blessings. Frankly, I'd like to keep him quiet."

"From what Mrs. Miller said, she and her husband don't communicate. I doubt either of them know how to talk to their child. A ventriloquist's dummy, something unthreatening, something that doesn't make judgments or criticize, may be exactly what Tony needs."

Halley stepped backward; Daniel moved closer.

"Tony's preadolescent. He's at the age when little boys start thinking about not-so-little girls." His grin widened.

She felt her shoulders touch the back wall. He'd neatly backed her into a corner, and he further trapped her by bracing his arms against the wall. The cloying cologne he wore offended her, and the smell of his breath almost made her think he'd been drinking. Halley ducked under his arm.

"If you don't mind, Dr. Daniels—" she began, but before she could get away, he caught her by the arm and spun her around. Their bodies collided. The man obviously didn't understand subtle protest. In a voice that could freeze rain, she said, "Kindly get your hands off me."

Before either of them could move Halley heard the door open behind them.

"Excuse me. I didn't know the room was occupied." She instantly recognized Mark's voice. "Mind if I use the candy machine?"

"Go right ahead," Daniel answered.

Halley twisted her head until she could see Mark. She could hear him jingling the change in his pocket. From his expression, it seemed that the only thing of importance taking place in the room was his deciding between a Snickers and a Babe Ruth!

Silently she cursed both doctors, Daniel for embarrassing her and Mark for being totally oblivious to her predicament.

But Mark wasn't oblivious. When he'd walked into the room and had seen them in a passionate clutch, he could have been a gentleman and politely excused himself. But Daniel had a reputation for making unwanted passes at new nurses. Should he pry them apart? That was what he wanted to do. But if Halley was exactly where she wanted to be, he'd be making a fool of himself with a brilliant show of machismo.

Alert for any sound of struggle, for any protest on her part, he stood ready to spin around and knock Daniel for a loop.

The lounge was quiet enough to hear a pin drop.

Mark's two quarters dropped into the candy machine. At the same time Halley ground the heel of her shoe on Daniel's big toe. He didn't release her, but she had the satisfaction of hearing him grunt. The candy bar dropped into the tray with a thud.

Mark picked up the candy, gave both of them a mock wave and departed. He'd given her an opportunity to protest. She hadn't. He sure wasn't going to stick around and watch them.

"Now we can get down to serious business," Daniel said, drawing her closer. "You're wild about me, aren't you?"

"I strongly suggest you remove your hands. Whoever gave you your broken nose is going to be thrilled to learn that I splatted it, too."

His fingers loosened enough for Halley to escape. "Don't you want me to agree to letting Tony—"

"Doctor, you may be a legend in your own mind, but you aren't in mine. Stay away from me. Do as you please regarding Tony. I won't be a pawn in any man's game."

"I was only kidding around a little," Daniel protested.

"I'm *not* kidding. Keep your distance." Halley moved through the door and slammed it for emphasis.

Jill, who was standing at the chart file, jumped. "Who lit your firecracker?"

"Dr. Edwards."

"Wasn't Mark just in there?"

Angry and humiliated, Halley snapped. "Do you honestly think one doctor would stop a member of the brotherhood while he was on the make? That would be unethical, my dear nurse."

Jill's eyes narrowed. "Daniel made a pass while Mark was there?"

"Never mind. Don't worry about it. I've had this kind of problem before and lived through it."

"You could make a formal complaint."

Halley laughed. "I did that once. I don't know who laughed harder, the hospital administrators, the doctors or the nurses. It's me. There must be something about me...."

"Maybe it's those tight pants you're wearing."

Halley ran her hands over her pastel blue slacks. They didn't feel tight. Her finger pulled out the side seam a good inch from her thigh. If anything, she'd lost four or five pounds the past week. She could ill afford to lose weight. Her pants were close to being baggy.

"Your oh-so-tight top, and revealing V neck that exposes your voluptuous cleavage might be..."

"You *are* joking," Halley said, chuckling, fingering the cowl neck of her blue and white top. "This shirt is fashionably *blousy*."

"Maybe it's your high-heeled shoes and silk stockings." Jill laughed as Halley faked a loud groan. "Regulation nurse's shoes and support stockings? Takes some kind of weirdo to find them a turn-on, huh?"

"Don't confuse me with logic. I'm the one recovering from hand-to-hand combat with an octopus. You're a blond bombshell. Why didn't Dr. Edwards corner you?"

"He did. Some men enjoy the hunt more than capturing the quarry. Once he knew I wanted to change his wicked ways by furnishing him with hearth and home, he fled." Jill tapped the eraser of her pencil on the counter top. "Daniel is handsome. He could be a damned fine doctor if he directed his energies toward the patients."

Halley looked at her skeptically.

"You're probably right. I'm carrying the angel of mercy image too far. Some men can't be rehabilitated."

Halley wondered if Mark fell into the same category. Renewed anger once again heightened her coloring. She didn't expect him to fight her battles. In fact, two doctors fighting over her was the last thing she wanted. But he could have stayed. Merely having another person in the room would have discouraged Dr. Edwards.

Her lips tightened into a straight line. *He thinks so little of me that he probably believes I was trying to seduce Dr. Edwards.*

"Your face is bright red," Jill observed. "You aren't coming down with something, are you?"

"Acute embarrassment mixed with rage. Nontreatable, but seldom chronic or debilitating," Halley reported as though entering the facts on a medical chart. "Mark witnessing Daniel's pass infuriates me."

"You weren't the only one infuriated. He snarled at Tammy when he strode toward the elevator. I'm beginning to wonder if he may be a woman hater."

"Yeah. Me in particular."

"You could explain."

Halley grimaced. It was no use. He'd twist her words until they made her look bad. "Why bother? He wouldn't believe me."

The phone buzzed. Jill picked it up. "Halley, it's for you." She cupped her hand over the receiver. "It's Mark."

Halley moved to take the call. "Nurse Twain speaking."

"I received a call from Dr. Edwards."

"Who's calling, please?" Halley asked coolly. What made him egotistical enough to believe she'd recognize his voice?

"Dr. Abraham."

The emphasis he gave the last syllable in his name clearly indicated he was aware of her needling him.

"Yes, sir. What can I do for you?"

Mark had all he could do to keep from telling her that she could conduct her intimate interlude where there wouldn't be a chance of his interrupting it.

"Edwards objects to Tony working with Oscar. He feels, and I quote, 'Excitement would be detrimental to his medical progress.' He doesn't want to be held responsible for a relapse."

"That's utterly ridiculous. What's a dummy going to do? Kick him in the knees and elbows?" she asked sarcastically.

"Professionally, my hands are tied. Tony is Daniel's patient."

Lowering her voice, Halley said, "That's a cop-out. We both know encouraging Tony's interest in a safe direction is an important aspect of his home-care management."

"Maybe you should try to convince Daniel to change his mind. Something tells me you'd have a better chance of success than I would."

Her voice shook with anger as she asked, "What do you mean?"

"Halley, I'm not blind." Mark forced a long-suffering tone into his voice to hid any trace of jealousy. "I saw you smooching with him."

"Smooching!"

"Whatever." Mark held his breath, fighting down the jealousy that clawed at his throat, waiting for her to deny what he'd seen.

Halley silently counted to ten. Screaming into the telephone while on duty would certainly get her a formal reprimand from Martha Chaney. Well then, if he was determined to think the worst, let him!

"Think a couple of lip locks will change his mind?" she inquired in a sultry voice, clenching her fist to keep a grip on her temper.

"Lip locks?"

"Kisses."

Mark inserted his finger between his starched collar and his neck. The thought of Halley kissing someone else, especially because he'd recommended it, had his heart thudding against his chest. He desperately wanted her to deny what he'd seen taking place in the lounge.

"Oh, well, uh . . ."

"Cat got your tongue?" Halley asked, purposely reminding him of the kiss they'd shared in his office by quoting Oscar.

"Perhaps the play therapist could convince Daniel."

Halley smiled. "I'll make a note of your recommendation on Tony's chart. Is there anything else?"

"Did anyone ever tell you that you have a sassy mouth?"

"I don't recall it being on my quarterly evaluations. Perhaps it's something you should discuss with my . . ."

"Supervising nurse," they both said simultaneously.

"You're skating on thin ice," Mark warned without malice, surprised to find himself grinning like an idiot.

"One cliché deserves another. Have you heard the one about fools rushing in where angels of mercy fear to tread? Maybe I'm a foolish angel."

"I don't suppose you'd like to tell me your version of what took place in the lounge."

A light flashing above Tony's door eliminated that possibility. "No. I've got to run. Bye."

Tony's raised voice carried into the hall. "You always stop me from doing anything fun! You did it because you hate me. You've always hated me!"

"I'll get Daniel," Jill said, rushing toward the lounge.

Within seconds Halley was in Tony's room. She was too late to stop him from yanking the phone off the nightstand and hurling it against the wall. Tears streamed from his eyes. His chest heaved. His arms flailed wildly.

Gently but firmly, Halley grasped his arms to restrain him from doing injury to himself. "Calm down, Tony. You're going to hurt yourself."

He went rigid beneath her hands, then collapsed against the pillow.

"Can you tell me what happened? I want to help you."

"Nobody can help me."

"We can try." Whatever was eating at Tony had to be brought out into the open. She lessened her grip. "Tell me. Please?"

"Dr. Edwards won't let me out of this stinking hospital because of *her*. He talked to me about learning how to work Dr. Abraham's dummy."

Halley released him when he paused, eyes searching for a tissue. Halley handed him several.

After wiping his eyes and blowing his nose, he babbled uncontrollably. "Dr. Edwards must have called my mother to get her permission. She refused! He called a few minutes ago to tell me I couldn't do it. I blasted Mom over the phone. She denied it, but she's covering up just like she used to do when I was a kid. I'd get a neat toy and it would disappear. She said she didn't take them, but I knew better. I know it's her fault I can't work the dummy. She's punishing me. It's her fault I have this disease and she hates me for it."

Tony spewed out so many problems at once that Halley didn't know which one to tackle first. She picked up Tony's hand to give herself a moment to think. The immediate problem had top priority. His distrust and doubts regarding his mother were deepseated. He'd need more help than a nurse could give him to deal with them.

"Your mother suggested having you learn how to work the dummy."

Tony turned his head away. "Don't lie."

"Listen to me, Tony. I never lie to patients. I was there when your mother and Dr. Abraham talked about it."

Daniel strode into the room. Jill followed with a medicine tray in her hand.

"Okay, Tony. It's time for your injection."

Tony squeezed Halley's fingertips. "What kind of shot? I don't usually get a shot now."

"Just a little something to calm you down," Daniel replied.

Halley shook her head. "Doctor, could I speak to you in the hall?"

"Of course. Jill, keep Tony as quiet as possible," Daniel instructed as he followed Halley from Tony's room.

"Tony doesn't need tranquilizers...depressants," Halley protested quietly. "He's been depressed since yesterday."

"Are you telling me how to treat my patient?"

"No, of course not." Halley realized, too late, Dr. Edwards had a double standard. Doctors didn't have to be tactful, but nurses did. A nurse could suggest methods of care, but telling him a patient didn't need medication he was prepared to administer was heresy. "Tony's upset about your refusal to let him learn how to operate the ventriloquist's dummy."

"I told you he was fragile," Daniel replied smugly, leaning closer to her.

Halley's eyes widened as she smelled his breath. He'd been drinking! She'd suspected it once before, and this time she was sure. How was she going to convince him to change his mind if he was under the influence of alcohol? His speech wasn't slurred, nor did he appear uncoordinated. Maybe he'd only had one or two drinks, she thought hopefully.

"You're right, Dr. Edwards. Tony is fragile. Mrs. Miller is also fragile. She's probably calling your office now. Tony called her after he talked to you."

Halley let that information sink into Daniel's thick head. She realized that Daniel must have called Tony from the nurses' lounge. Her opinion of him sank lower. Daniel was too cowardly even to face a boy! Her eyes narrowed. If Daniel couldn't say no to Tony, could he face Mrs. Miller's wrath?

"Mrs. Miller thought the ventriloquist's dummy would be beneficial for her son," Halley said slowly. "It was her idea."

Dismay showed clearly in Daniel's face. "Mark volunteered his help. He didn't say anything about Mrs. Miller," Daniel said. Muttering to himself, he added, "I can't let another doctor build a rapport..."

"Is that what you're going to tell Tony's mother?" Halley asked innocently. Mrs. Miller was probably livid, and Daniel might soon be faced with the choice of correcting his error in judgment or losing a patient to another doctor. Halley didn't care which he chose. For that matter, he could lose his entire practice and she wouldn't care one iota.

"No, and you aren't going to say anything either! Tony can have his stupid dummy! I'll straighten everything out with Mrs. Miller."

"What about the tranquilizer?"

"You nurses complain about his temper tantrums, then get upset about a mild sedative," he snapped. "Women!"

She didn't have an answer, but she felt confident Tony wouldn't get the shot. Breathing a sigh of relief, she followed Daniel back into the boy's room.

He dismissed Jill and the medical tray with a casual wave of his hand.

"Well, now, young man. It looks like you've calmed down considerably. There seems to be some misunderstanding about the dummy. When I mentioned it earlier, I noticed how excited you became. But, after reconsidering, I think my suggesting it to your mother a while back was a solid idea.''

Halley cringed inwardly. *He suggested it! The lousy rat is taking credit for the idea at Mrs. Miller's expense.* Every nerve ending in her body screamed for her to make Daniel tell the truth. Tony's mother deserved the credit.

She bit her lip to keep from antagonizing Dr. Edwards. What would telling the truth accomplish? Daniel might simply change his mind and they'd be back where they started. Wisely, Halley kept her mouth shut.

''Does that mean . . .'' Tony's eyes lit up.

''*If* you don't overexcite yourself, I think it's a fine idea.''

''Thanks, Doc. My mom won't change your mind, will she?''

Daniel chuckled. ''I'll be my most persuasive.''

I'll bet your silver tongue will have to work overtime to fast-talk Mrs. Miller.

''Halley, I'll let you make the arrangements with Dr. Abraham.'' He beamed a toothy smile at Tony. ''Who knows? You may be a budding ventriloquist, a future Hollywood star. You'll sign an autographed picture for me, won't you?'' he asked jovially.

''Yeah! I can hardly wait!'' Tony replied, squirming.

''See you tomorrow morning.''

Halley glared at Daniel's back as he departed.

''Halley, would you plug the phone back in for me? I'm going to call the library and see if they have any books I can read about ventriloquism. After Dr. Edwards talks to Mom, I'll have her stop by the library and pick them up.''

As she left the room, Tony was laughing and chatting with the librarian. She could hardly wait to talk to Mark. They'd won! Sometimes it was the little victories, like hearing a child laugh, that counted.

Feeling lighthearted she returned to the nurses' station. The three o'clock shift had arrived, which meant she'd be giving her reports orally. And, as usual, she'd be late leaving. Her feet ached and her legs were tired, but she didn't mind. She felt good about herself and her job.

Chapter Five

Off duty, eager to share the good news, Halley briskly strode from the hospital to the professional quadrangle. She could have called and let Mark's receptionist tell him to bring Oscar tomorrow morning on early-morning rounds. She didn't. Selfishly, she wanted to see Mark's face light up, his frown disappear. Maybe he'd give her one of his rare smiles without Oscar's prompting.

As she entered Mark's waiting room, a mother and her two small children were being escorted by the receptionist into the examination room. Shortly, the receptionist returned.

"Can I help you?" Lu Anne asked.

"I'd like to see Dr. Abraham when he's finished."

"Do you have an appointment?"

"No."

Lu Anne slid a clipboard with a standard patient history form through the receptionist's window. "Would you fill this out, please? Dr. Abraham will be able to see you and your—" She glanced downward, looking for a child. Her brow creased with puzzlement. "Isn't your child with you?"

Halley smiled. "I'm not here for medical reasons."

"Oh?"

The elongated vowel seemed to hold a wealth of questions and the speculative look in the receptionist's eyes as she did a quick physical inventory made Halley reconsider leaving a message.

"I'm Halley Twain, one of the pediatric nurses from St. Michael's." The receptionist's raised eyebrow was more expressive than her seemingly limited vocabulary. "I'm here about a patient."

"Which patient?"

"Tony Miller."

Lu Anne reached for the patient roster. "I don't recall Dr. Abraham mentioning a Tony Miller."

"He isn't exactly Mark's patient." Halley watched the receptionist's eyebrow climb higher. "He's Dr. Edwards's patient."

"Oh?"

Mark's receptionist certainly didn't waste words. Each "oh" was meant to elicit further information, but Halley wasn't in the mood for long, involved explanations. She was there to talk to Mark, not his female bodyguard.

"Lu Anne..." Mark halted between the examining room and Lu Anne's office when he saw Halley. His dark eyes lit with surprise. Daniel had already called him and reluctantly told him that he and Oscar now had visiting privileges with Tony. Was she here to gloat over convincing Daniel to agree? Her grin matched the one on Garfield's face behind her. He couldn't see even a trace of smugness.

"I have to leave now, if that's okay," Lu Anne said. She returned the roster and picked up her purse. "Tommy's teacher said she couldn't wait past four o'clock."

Mark was in a bind. He had two squirmy children to inoculate, a squeamish mother and no one to assist him. Lu Anne was making fast tracks toward the door before he could detain her. Much as he disliked asking favors, it would be extremely difficult to give the shots without help. He strode to the communicating door and opened it.

"Would you mind helping me?"

"Not at all." Halley walked toward him, shrugging out of her coat. His hands barely touched her shoulders as he courteously assisted her, but her heart still fluttered. She couldn't look at him for fear of what he could read in her eyes. One touch—that was all it took to destroy her defenses.

He hung her coat next to his on the brass coat tree. The satin lining was still warm from her body heat, and her fragrance clung to the coat, reminding him of spring flowers and gentle rains. A tremor ran through his hands. He had to fight the urge to bury his nose in the soft material, and revel in her beguiling fragrance.

He swallowed hard. Halley would certainly have reason to gloat, he thought, if she had any idea how her mere scent stirred his senses. She could make a strong man weak with her innocent smiles. He had to be careful, very careful around her.

"Joyce Lawson, Mindy and Jack's mother, is like a brick when there's an emergency, but she faints at the sight of a needle. If you'll just sort of hug little Mindy, I'll do the rest. Jack is a trooper. He always sets a good example for his sister."

Her mouth too dry for speech, Halley nodded, waiting for Mark to lead the way.

He turned toward the refrigerator where the perishable serums were stored. "They're waiting in the second room on your right. I'll be there in a minute."

Halley could hear Mindy and Jack discussing the merits of choosing a ring over choosing an eraser shaped like a cat from the doctor's goodie box. Quietly she entered the room and introduced herself to Mrs. Lawson.

"Hi!" Jack, the older of the two children, said as he closed his fists. "Pick a hand."

Halley tapped his left hand, and his fingers uncurled. A ring twinkled in the palm of Jack's hand. "If you're brave and don't scream and yell, you get to keep it."

"What if *you* scream and yell? Do I still get to keep it?" Halley asked, ruffling his reddish hair.

"I never scream." He shot his three-year-old sister a dirty look. "She's a baby. She screams."

"Do not!" Mindy argued, pouting her lower lip. "I'm a big girl!"

Jack pressed the ring into Halley's hand. "I'm almost a man."

"Me, too! Huh, Mommie?" The little girl climbed into her mother's lap, her thumb in her mouth. She busily twisted a lock of her fair hair around her forefinger.

"Only babies suck their thumbs," Jack jeered.

Mrs. Lawson hugged Mindy and rolled her eyes toward the ceiling. "That's enough, children."

Halley flipped on the examination light and turned it toward the wall. "There's a rabbit in here," she whispered, drawing their attention to the shadow her fingers cast on the wall. Her fist formed the head. As she raised her little finger and forefinger, the rabbit grew ears. The fleshy tip of her thumb made a nose.

"His nose is wiggling, Mommy!" Mindy squealed with delight. "Make his ears flop."

The shadow of her finger bent. "I hear wings flapping. There must be birds around. See if you can tell me what kind of bird." She twisted one arm over the other.

"Swan! I can tell by its long neck," Jack said.

"And this?" Hooking her thumbs together and spreading her fingers like wings, she created the image of a large, flying bird.

"Eagle?" Jack asked, trying to imitate the position of her hands. "Show me how to do it."

"Sure. Mindy, do you want to make a bird?"

"Yes!"

Halley showed Jack how to place his hands, then picked Mindy up and showed her. Both children laughed and squealed, their hands darting between the light and the wall. Soon they had totally forgotten why they were in the office.

"I wanna make a wabbit!" Mindy demanded.

"Can do," Halley said enthusiastically, showing Mindy how to hold her hand.

"My bird is going to get your wabbit," Jack yelled, his hands swooping downward.

Over Mindy's shoulder, Halley watched Mark enter the room. A broad smile made his face look incredibly handsome. "You've changed my office into a zoo!"

"I can make a wabbit," Mindy announced, eager to share her trick. "Wanna see?"

"Uh-huh. You make a rabbit while I tend to you. Okay?" Mark always told his young patients what to expect. "This is going to sting but only for a second. You let Miss Bunny Rabbit say 'Ouch.'"

"Ouch!"

"Not yet, Mindy." Mark winked at Halley as he tugged at Mindy's frilly panties.

Halley hugged the little girl. "Make both ears flop."

In an instant Mark was finished. "I didn't hear Miss Bunny Rabbit."

"She's a brave wabbit, isn't she?" Mindy asked proudly. "She didn't cry or anything."

"She's superbrave," Mark agreed. He lifted her from Halley's arms, hugged her and sat her on her mother's lap. "Superbrave. How about your eagle, Jack?"

Looking only slightly nervous, Jack climbed on the examination table with a helping boost up from Mark. Looping one arm around Halley's neck, he whispered, "You can keep the ring."

"Are you giving away my precious rings?" Mark teased.

"The purple diamond matches her eyes. She has *real* pretty eyes."

Mark grinned, preparing the hypodermic. "Purple diamond? You picked out an expensive one. Ready?"

"Uh-huh." Jack grimaced, then snuggled his face against Halley's chest. He stuck out his arm. "Ready."

Halley watched Mark intently as she hugged Jack. A second before he administered the injection, their eyes met. They shared a special feeling that occasionally passes between a doctor and a nurse. Although it sent a tingling sensation up her spine and a warm glow to her cheeks, it wasn't sexual. It was like a gentle touching of souls.

"Jack whispered 'ouch,'" Mindy chortled to her mother. "I heard him."

"Did not!"

Mrs. Lawson chuckled. "Everything's back to normal. Has modern medicine discovered anything to cure sibling rivalry?"

"Time is a great cure-all." Mark dropped the disposable syringe into the trash basket. "Bickering is normal for children their age. Don't worry about it."

"I suppose I'll get over it in ten or fifteen years. I think I'd rather take a shot," Mrs. Lawson quipped. "Okay, my brave eagle and rabbit, let's go."

"I'm hungry. Do we get to go to McDonald's?" Jack asked, spreading his arms and winging out the door.

Mindy hopped after him. "Pizza, Mommy. I want pizza. No hamburgers!"

Shaking her head, Mrs. Lawson followed. "Thanks, Dr. Abraham. You, too, Halley. Night."

"I'll straighten up while you let them out," Halley offered.

"Don't bother. I've imposed enough."

"No bother." Halley gave him a gentle shove. "Go."

Thinking how well they'd worked together, Halley ripped off the sheet of paper covering the examination table. She'd done little more than provide comfort, but that was an important part of nursing. Turning off the examination light, she glanced around the room, looking for instruments that weren't properly stored. Everything was in place.

"They're a handful, aren't they?" Mark asked, leaning against the inside of the doorjamb. He'd removed his white lab coat and loosened his tie.

To Halley, the room suddenly seemed to shrink. She hoped Mark couldn't hear her heart pounding. "They were great."

"Thanks for your help. It was above and beyond duty with those little rascals."

In the few seconds their eyes had met and held, Mark felt closer to Halley than he'd ever felt to any woman. She radiated a deep inner beauty. If only...

"What are you thinking?" Halley asked, unable to figure out why his smile had frozen.

"Nothing." *Everything! Why does she have to be so beautiful?*

"This morning, Tony gave me the same answer. Three hours later he was throwing a conniption fit. I've had my quota of tantrums for the day, so why don't you tell me what's bothering you?" She moved from behind the examination table. She'd failed to get her patient to talk. One failure a day was one too many and Halley wasn't going to leave until she'd pried Mark's mouth open. "We've agreed to disagree about

Jason. Is there something else you're holding against me?''

He scowled. The thought of complaining to Halley about her beauty was ludicrous. Other men would be praising it, not silently criticizing it.

He had to keep his thoughts private.

"Daniel called."

"He's enough to make Oscar frown," Halley muttered. She considered telling Mark about smelling liquor on Daniel's breath. Only her doubt that he wouldn't believe her kept her silent.

"Daniel agreed to the Oscar idea."

"That's today's good news. In fact, that's what I came here to tell you. But I won't be sidetracked, Mark. From our first meeting in the elevator when you rhymed my name with alley, we've been brawling like alley cats. Today, I'll admit, I wanted to scratch out your eyes."

"Daniel, again?" Mark plowed his fingers through his hair. "I walked into the lounge and saw—"

"Daniel making a pass."

"I didn't hear you scream."

"A brave wabbit doesn't scream 'ouch,'" she retorted dryly.

Mindy's words brought a lopsided smile to his lips. "A brave rabbit isn't a dumb bunny. She's smart enough not to twitch her cute little powder-puff tail in front of a wolf."

"And what should Eagle Eyes do when he flies over and sees the wolf pawing the rabbit? Stick a candy bar in his beak and soar into the sky?"

"You'd feel safer in the clutches of an eagle than a wolf?" Mark bantered, the edge of his ill humor dulled by her wit.

Halley laid her hand on his arm. "I'd have felt safer if the eagle had circled for a while. I could have cheerfully murdered you for acting as though I was filling a medical order."

"Acting. That's precisely what I was doing," Mark admitted. "I figured you were hunting other quarry and I shouldn't interfere."

"Jason's lies are sticking in your craw, aren't they?"

Her hand dropped as Mark simply turned and walked slowly down the hall. For a moment she despaired of ever convincing him of the truth. Jason was a habitual liar and an exceptionally convincing one. Accomplished liars, like poisonous spiders, could spin intricate gossamer webs. Unsuspecting prey, like Mark and herself, were captured and paralyzed before they knew what happened. Extricating herself from Jason's web had been a long, painful procedure, and she doubted she had the stamina to pull Mark out of the same web.

Mark walked into the waiting room. He couldn't think straight with her touching him. His flesh under her palm had burned. Making a noise that was a cross between a snort and a laugh, he remembered what he'd told Martha: burn victims seldom play with matches a second time. And yet, here he was fascinated by Halley.

He sank into a chair. Elbows on his bent knees, he held his head in his hands. Jason had painted Halley's character the blackest of blacks. He'd said she was a party girl, a sexy bed partner who'd kept him awake all night satisfying herself. According to him, she was a nurse who saw marriage as early retirement. Blacker than black, he thought, rubbing the heels of his hands against his eyes.

What he'd heard from Jason and what he'd witnessed himself were diametrically opposed. With Tony, Mindy and Jack, Halley had been terrific. She genuinely cared about children in the ward, and she meticulously performed all the tedious chores expected of a nurse. Professionally, he couldn't find fault with her. A nurse who worked overtime and went to extra lengths to care for children was dedicated to her profession.

Could Jason's lover and Halley Twain be the same person?

Mark dropped his hands, blinking his eyes. Halley had quietly seated herself on the sofa across from him. He had to hear her side of the story. Not knowing was driving him crazy.

"What Jason said does stick in my craw," Mark admitted.

"Then it's time to perform an emergency tracheotomy." Halley bent toward Mark, leveling her eyes with his. "Now that you're going to listen, I don't know where to begin."

"At the beginning."

Halley hesitated an instant then started to speak. "I saw Jason for the first time at my twin sister's bedside. Kate had cystic fibrosis. Jason was in premed at the time, working in the hospital lab part-time. I was graduating from high school the next day."

Mark nodded. Disease intensification of a cystic fibrosis patient often coincided with special social events and holidays. He wondered what effects Halley's twin's illness had on her life, but he didn't interrupt.

"I assumed he was a doctor, a young genius consulting with Kate's doctor." Halley grimaced at her naïveté. "He didn't correct my error. Kate was sicker than the devil with bronchiolitis, but Jason's presence seemed to be helping her more than the medication. I remember feeling glad that Jason was flirting outrageously with her. Kate missed so much in her short life."

Halley rose to her feet, unable to sit any longer. "Kate died during my last year in nurse's training. I was already working at St. Michael's when Jason's path crossed mine again. Romantic fate—I remember thinking that at the time. By then, he was graduating from medical school. In gratitude for his kindness to my sister, I laughed off his pretending to be Kate's consultant years before. We dated occasionally, nothing serious.

"Back then, I had more money than sense." Halley sighed over her stupidity. "Jason gave me a song and dance about slaving away at the hospital and having almost no money. I fell for his sob story and offered to let him move in with me. Strictly a platonic relationship, I thought. But that's not what Jason expected. I soothed his worried brow, cooked his meals, washed his clothes, paid the bills and, eventually, he charmed me into sharing his bed. When he accepted an internship at St. Michael's, I tagged along with him. I'd heard snatches of gossip that had me wondering, but—I was just plain stupid."

"Love can do that," Mark muttered, empathizing with her. He'd been a prize fool himself.

"Anyway, the closer Jason came to completing internship, the farther we drifted apart. He started staying out late almost every night. When I confronted him, he admitted to 'carousing.' His word, not mine."

She could give Mark the bare facts, but she couldn't tell him Jason's reasoning behind his actions. Jason's opinion that she was less than an enthusiastic partner in bed was too humiliating to reveal.

"We fought continually. He promised the moon, then kicked dirt in my face. After a while, I didn't know whether I was coming or going. Jason specialized in pinpointing my weaknesses and exploiting them to his benefit. Finally, I couldn't take it any longer and I packed my bags. He threatened to drop his internship if I walked out. I'd already had my share of guilt feelings over my sister's death. So I took his verbal abuse rather than risk being responsible for something happening to him. He completed his internship, as you know, by the skin of his teeth."

Her back stiffened as she recalled the final insult. "He threw a wild party before he left. Weren't you invited?"

"Probably, but I'm not a socialite."

Her hands balled into a fist. Jason's final dose of humiliation had been administered in public. Tears of shame burned her eyes. "But you heard about it, didn't you?"

"I avoid listening to gossip."

"The gossip couldn't possibly have been worse than the truth." She wiped away the lone tear trickling down her cheek. "By midnight, the party had all the symptoms of turning into a drunken orgy. I had retreated to the kitchen, but Jason made up some lie about a spilled drink to get me into the living room.''

"That's enough," Mark said through clenched teeth. "I don't want to hear any more."

Halley shook her head. Tears she didn't realize she'd shed dripped from her face. She scrubbed them away with her fingertips.

"No. You're going to listen. You're going to find out why I hate Jason Malone with every bone in my body."

Mark started to rise from his chair. Halley, still standing, put her hands on his shoulder and pushed him backward. She held him there.

"He had a special surprise farewell gift for me. In front of his leering buddies, he announced who his replacement would be...'my new live-in lover.''' Her voice dropped until it was barely audible. "He made a laughingstock out of me before I could break his grip and run out of the room."

"Oh, Halley...Halley, I'm so sorry." He gently pulled her onto his lap, framing her face with his hands, wiping away her tears with his thumbs.

Her arms braced against his chest, the last thing she wanted was pity. "I don't want you to feel sorry for me. I transferred out of ER to escape the sympathetic looks. Please, no pity! All I want from you is an end to the hostilities Jason caused. I'm a good nurse. Yes, I'm a lousy judge of men; I picked a loser. But I'm good at my job."

"Cry, Halley," he encouraged. Her valiant effort to remain calm moved Mark. She really didn't want sympathy. She wanted his respect. "Cry. Get it out of your system," he murmured.

"Don't misunderstand. Jason Malone didn't break my heart. He damaged my pride." She plucked a tissue from the box on the end table. Rubbing her eyes, she wished she were one of those women who could bawl without their noses turning beet-red and their eyes getting bloodshot. "I'm not crying over Jason. I was over him long before he left. He's gone from my life and I'm glad."

"Frankly, I'd like to punch his lights out," Mark said vehemently.

A thrill of pleasure coursed through Halley. Mark believed her, and even better than that, he wanted to champion her cause.

The hint of a smile curving her lips disappeared when she heard him say, "I tolerated his slipups. Covered for him. He's a licensed physician with minimal skills."

To keep him from observing her disappointment, she wiggled off his lap. Leave it to Mark to worry about the long-range effects on the medical profession, she thought. The possibility that the sacred brotherhood might suffer was far worse than her being hurt.

"Don't worry," she said reassuringly. "Jason is motivated by money. He'll perform adequately."

"Sick patients need more than adequate care. Which reminds me." He glanced at his watch. "I have evening rounds to make."

Halley didn't need to be told twice. She strode to the coatrack. "Here's your coat. The temperature dropped twenty degrees today."

"Thanks."

He helped Halley put on her coat, carefully to avoid touching her. She'd bared her soul to him. He wasn't the sort of man who took advantage of a vulnerable woman. He'd cleverly switched from the personal to the professional when he could no longer stand the intimate warmth of her thighs against his. He could control his primitive instincts. He wasn't a swine.

A small tenor voice inside him said, "Oink-oink."

Mark glanced at Oscar's trunk.

"Shut up!" he muttered, and joined Halley as she exited.

Chapter Six

To Halley's way of thinking, the only thing worse than eating alone was cooking for one person. She stood in front of a wide array of beef, pork and chicken at the grocery store. The choice of eating the same kind of meat for five days straight, or fixing yet another frozen dinner dulled her appetite. She resigned herself to another frozen dinner.

"The butcher must weigh a ton or have ten kids," she muttered, basing her observation on the amount of meat in each of the packages.

"Less than a week in pediatrics and you're talking to yourself?"

Halley turned.

Martha Chaney's basket rolled next to hers. "You know what they call people who talk to themselves?"

"Either a ventriloquist or a dummy," Halley joked, refusing to give the stock answer: crazy. She noticed Martha's cart was filled with frozen dinners. "Do you live alone?"

"Yeah. My youngest child flew from the nest last month. The rest of the kids are scattered hither and yonder." Martha pushed her glasses up the bridge of her nose with her thumb, a sure sign that she was annoyed. "Five kids and I live alone. I've been a widow for years."

Halley grinned. "Single life isn't what it's cracked up to be, is it?"

"It's awful."

Giggling, Halley suggested a cure for their common problem. "I fix a mean plate of linguine and clam sauce. Care to join me for dinner?"

"I toss a wicked salad," Martha replied, matching Halley's grin. "My place or yours?"

"Mine. You pick up the salad fixings and I'll meet you at the checkout counter." Realizing she was bossing her boss, she added, "If that's okay with you."

"It's an offer too tempting to refuse. Incidentally, I have a strict policy about fraternizing with the nurses. I don't." She wheeled her cart toward the fresh vegetables. "But I'm so hungry for a decent meal and a little company that I'll have to make an exception. Guess we'll have to be friends, won't we?"

"I'd like that," Halley agreed, pushing her cart toward the dried foods aisle. Two new friends in a day was a record breaker for a woman who could count all her friends on one hand, and still have enough fingers lift over to twirl linguine on a fork.

Within the hour, Halley juggled a grocery sack
while unlocking the front door of her apartment.
"Welcome to my abode—such as it is," she said,
pushing the door wide open. "The kitchen is straight
ahead."

Martha's eyes widened with pleasure as she glanced
around Halley's living room.

"Not what you expected?" Halley asked, amused.
"No chrome. No glass."

"Solid oak furniture and colorful, practical, cot-
ton prints. Our decorating taste is similar," Martha
responded, pleased. Intrigued by the handmade objects displayed in the corner cabinets, Martha moved
closer. Pointing to a carved white swan, she said, "I've
been looking for one of those. Where did you get it?"

"Lake of the Ozarks, in Missouri. I'm a pushover
for artsy-craftsy knicknacks, especially carved wood.
Tenants here aren't allowed to have pets, so I make do
with stroking my carvings."

"Surely, a girl as young and pretty as you are can
find something better to touch," Martha teased, following Halley into the kitchen.

Unloading the groceries, Halley avoided the compliment, choosing her words carefully. "Wooden
carvings last forever."

"As do love and friendship, if *both* people involved take care of it. Even artwork can suffer from
neglect." Martha took the salad makings to the cutting board. With a nonchalance that made Halley
suspicious, she said, "You and Mark must be getting
along well."

"The salad bowl is in the right-hand cabinet beside
the refrigerator."

"I think Tony's depression revolved around being in the hospital during the holidays. Since you and Mark convinced Daniel to let Tony work with Oscar, his whole attitude has changed," Martha said while dicing the celery. "I've been so worried about Jimmy Owens finding a kidney donor, before it's too late, that I haven't pampered Tony as much as I should. Daniel doesn't pamper him, either."

Halley pulled a five-quart pot from the butcher block in the center of the kitchen. As she filled it with hot water, she considered telling Martha about smelling liquor on Daniel's breath. Of course she had no way of knowing if Daniel had actually been drunk or had simply had had one drink. What she *did* know, however, was that practicing medicine while under the influence of alcohol was strictly forbidden. Being new to the pediatric ward made her hesitate. She didn't want the reputation of being a trouble-maker. She set the pot on the back burner of the stove and turned the burner on. While the water was heating, she began to fix the clam sauce.

"What do you think of Daniel?" Halley finally asked.

"He wouldn't know the difference between an expensive wooden carving and a Kewpie doll," Martha answered with characteristic bluntness. She removed the outside leaves of the head of lettuce, rinsed it, then began tearing it in bite-size pieces. A wry smile curved her lips. "Now Mark, on the other hand, has a prize carving of sorts—Oscar."

"I think Mark would resent your calling Oscar a carving," Halley replied evasively.

"To quote Mark, 'Oscar is a dummy.' Sometimes, though, I think Oscar is smarter than Mark. People-smart. Do you know what I mean?"

Halley chuckled. "Martha, Oscar *is* Mark!"

"Oscar is such a little rascal. Every time he opens his mouth the unexpected pops out. When Mark speaks for himself he has a filter between his brain and his mouth. When he speaks through Oscar he's totally uninhibited. If he thinks it, he says it."

"Do you think Mark is a bit bashful?"

"Where's the carrot scraper?"

"In the drawer by your right hand."

"No, I think Mark was probably a late bloomer socially. He didn't marry until he was in his early thirties. Unlike your wooden carvings, Mark wasn't given sufficient care. The marriage cracked within a year."

While peeling and dicing an onion, Halley mentally stored each morsel of information regarding Mark. Tears gathered in her eyes. She seldom cried even when dicing onions, but lately it seemed as if her tear ducts were working overtime. First, when she was sitting on Mark's lap, she had to blink to keep tears of self-pity from falling, and now, she had all she could do to hold them back because of Mark's unfortunate marriage. The thought of Mark being neglected, left on a shelf, bothered her.

Martha noticed Halley wiping her eyes and handed her a paper towel. "Rinse your hands, then wet the towel and dab your eyes."

Casting Martha a watery smile, Halley followed her instructions. Once her eyes were dry, she asked, "How much garlic do you like in your sauce?"

"Lots. It keeps the werewolves away. Not that I have to worry about male wolves—weird or not."

"You're an attractive woman," Halley asserted, grinning as she peeled several cloves of garlic. "With or without garlic, any wolf with half a brain would pursue you."

Martha sliced a tomato into thin wedges. She eyed Halley up and down, then pushed her glasses back in place.

"What's bothering you?" Halley asked, recognizing the gesture.

"I was thinking about something Mark said before you started working in pediatrics."

"Mark knew I'd asked for a transfer?"

Martha nodded. "Um-hmm. Actually, he was against . . . Oooops!"

Halley finished the words Martha had stopped with the palm of her hand. "Against my transfer? It's okay, Martha. Jason Malone did a hatchet job on me. Mark and I straightened out that problem."

"Thought I'd put my foot in my mouth," Martha said, heaving a sigh of relief. "I can't see any resemblance between you and Cleo."

For a second, Halley was lost. Was Cleo Mark's ex-wife? Curious, certain Martha would stop talking if she realized how much she was divulging, Halley opened the refrigerator and ducked her head inside it.

"Cleo's beautiful, and an ex-nurse—other than that, I don't see any similarities." Martha glanced over her shoulder toward Halley. "Did we forget something?"

"Here it is." Holding a stick of butter in her hand, Halley straightened and closed the refrigerator.

"I thought I was going to have to treat your nose for frostbite," Martha joked. "Where was I?"

Halley unwrapped the butter and dropped it into a skillet. Martha had given her an opportunity to change the subject, but she found herself wanting to know more about Mark's mysterious ex-wife. In particular, she wanted to know why he thought she was like Cleo. Perhaps Jason's lies weren't the only reason she'd been subjected to Mark's animosity, after all.

"You were telling me about Cleo and Mark."

"I don't think any woman can speak with authority about someone like Cleo. She's a femme fatale—a man's woman." Martha groaned and glanced upward. "Forgive me, Mother."

Halley laughed. "What does your mother have to do with Cleo?"

"Girlhood promise. My mother objected to anything being said that wasn't nice." Her voice dropped. "If I strictly adhered to the rule, I wouldn't be able to mouth Cleo's name."

"That bad?"

"Worse. Cleo had a way of making everyone, including the patients, feel as though they were covered with warts. Warts with hairs," Martha added for good measure. "And, being a nurse, Cleo knew how to remove warts effectively: freeze them off with icy haughtiness, burn them off with her hot temper or cut them off with a sharp tongue. But ... she was charming with the doctors, Mark in particular."

"It surprises me that Mark would fall for her. He's certainly wary of women now."

She'd watched Mark with the other nurses. He was polite, but distant. He rarely spoke, other than to give information regarding a patient. The nurses obviously found him very attractive, but he was indifferent.

Mark's behavior toward her vacillated between anger and passion, never indifference. At one point, Halley would have welcomed his treating her as he did the other nurses. Since their earthshaking kiss, she'd begrudgingly found herself wanting more than equal treatment. She wanted a great deal more than courtesy and respect. Was she looking for physical satisfaction? she silently asked herself.

No, despite the odds against her, she still wanted what they'd spoken of...the impossible dream. Love. This time she wouldn't make the mistake of settling for less.

Martha snorted, drawing Halley from her thoughts.

"Cleo flattered him. Made him feel as though he was ten feet tall, built like Paul Bunyan, with the personality of Bob Hope. Believe me, Halley, she was a classic witch. A sexy witch around men, a sarcastic witch around women. Their marriage fell apart before their first anniversary." Martha made a dismissing gesture. "'Nuff said about Cleo. Otherwise, I'll spoil my dinner."

Halley put the onion, garlic and clams into the sizzling butter and added a few pinches of Italian spices. Inhaling the pungent aroma, she said, "Don't spoil your appetite. I'll gain ten pounds eating this by myself."

"Smells heavenly," Martha agreed. "I'll make the salad dressing and set the table while you put the finishing touches on the linguine sauce."

Minutes later, they swirled linguine on their forks.

Halley took a bite. Her lips closed, she savored the sauce. "What do you think?"

"You're going to make some man very, very lucky. How'd you like to meet my nineteen-year-old son?" Martha teased, half kidding and half serious. "I'll fix you up, arrange the wedding and eat Sunday dinners at your house!"

"No, thanks," Halley said with a laugh. "You'd make a great mother-in-law, but I'm not into younger men."

A gleam entered Martha's eyes. "You might be interested in my unofficially adopted son. He's mature, good-looking, wonderful, patient, caring, financially secure, great sense of humor..."

"Stop! Your linguine will get cold while you're listing his attributes!" Halley laughed as she watched Martha put her fork on her plate and rub her hands together. "When do I meet this paragon of virtue?"

"I fixed you up with him once. Don't you remember?"

Halley shook her head. "Martha, you've never fixed me up with anyone."

Rolling her eyes to the ceiling, Martha gave a mock groan. "Oh, how soon these young ones forget," she complained. "Don't you remember your Thanksgiving party assignment?"

"Oscar?"

"Mmm," Martha replied, chewing thoughtfully. She swallowed. "My, my, my, Halley. You are forgetful. You're the one who reminded me that Mark and Oscar are one and the same. Isn't Mark everything I described?"

"Were you playing matchmaker?" Halley demanded, slightly appalled.

"Answer my question. Isn't Mark Abraham everything I described?"

"You'd fire me if I said no," Halley said teasingly, watching Martha anxiously lean forward.

"Probably."

"Well, in that case, I have no choice. Dr. Mark Abraham is perfect."

Martha grinned cherubically. "I'll tell him what you said."

"Don't you dare!" She dropped her fork and reached across the table for Martha's plate. "You've had your last bite of linguine if it's going to make your tongue wag!"

"Touch that plate and I'll rap your knuckles," Martha threatened, laughing, obviously pleased with Halley's reaction. "My lips are sealed."

"Don't count your Sunday dinners before they're cooked. Mark and I are no longer keeping score on who can be the ugliest, but we're a long way from Sunday dinners." Remembering how angry Mark was over the lies that enabled Jason to finish his internship, she added, "Oscar says Mark is a workaholic, who's happily married to the medical profession. I tend to agree."

"Oscar says what Mark wants you to hear. He's been hurt. You're a nurse . . . fix him!" Martha ate a mouthful of salad.

"Heart transplants are relatively simple compared to mending a broken heart. That's complicated."

Martha patted Halley's hand. "Delicate, not complicated. He'll respond to TLC."

"I'll put that on his medical record, Nurse Chaney. Speaking of medical records—" Halley pointedly changed the direction of the conversation "—tell me about Jimmy Owens's family background."

"As you know, he's Mark's patient. Of course, a kidney specialist is involved, but Jimmy relies on Mark."

"He's five, right?" Martha nodded. "No brothers or sisters?"

"No, Jimmy's mother and father, Lila and Phil, want more children, but they're afraid Jimmy's degenerative disease is hereditary. So far we haven't been able to locate a donor. No matchups in the family. No matchups so far on the computer."

"My sister had cystic fibrosis that wasn't detected until after my brother and younger sister were born. The whole time we were growing up, if one of us had a mild case of the sniffles, my parents were upset."

"That's something an outsider has trouble understanding. The sick child is often less of a burden than the weight of the family's anxieties and guilt feelings. I imagine, since your sister was a twin, you had your share of the burden."

"Yeah. I kept asking myself, 'Why her? Why not me?' At other times, I'd thank God I wasn't sick, then feel guilty for being well."

"Compassion comes from working through those conflicting emotions."

"Our family worked with a superb counselor." Seeing that talking about Jimmy was beginning to bother Martha, she said, "I read an interesting article in one of the medical journals about nurses interacting with counselors."

Halley and Martha exchanged ideas while polishing off their meal. Then they polished off the dishes. By nine-thirty, both of them were sitting on the couch, rubbing their sore feet and stifling yawns.

"I'm still stuffed," Martha groaned, rising to her feet. "If I don't get in my car and drive home, I'll be sound asleep within the hour."

"Sure you don't want a cup of coffee?"

"No room." Martha ran a hand over her ample hips. "Thanks for dinner and the company."

"My pleasure."

"Are you certain you don't want me to fix you up with my son? He's wild about Italian food."

Halley laughed. "We'll have to do this again, soon."

"After the holidays, we'll have a bachelorette party at my house. Good night. Thanks again."

Closing the door, Halley locked it, then crossed to her bedroom. She stretched. Her legs and feet ached, as usual. With each step, she lazily unbuttoned her blouse, turning off the lights as she went.

Halley might have furnished dinner, but Martha had certainly given her food for thought.

The fact that Mark had objected to her transfer wasn't news. But, until she'd spoken to Martha, she'd assumed his objection had been based solely on Jason's lies. Confident that Mark no longer thought of her as the destructive force in Jason's professional career, she wondered what continued to cause the tension between them.

Was Cleo, his ex-wife, the root of the friction?

Martha hadn't made any bones about disliking Cleo's femme fatale ways, but could that be just sour

grapes? Halley immediately discounted that possibility. Martha couldn't care less what others thought of
her appearance. Standing in front of the mirror in her
bra and panties, Halley wished she could say the same.

"Lust and distrust," Halley said aloud, summariz-
ing her own problem.

Men lusted and women distrusted her.

Halley unsnapped her bra and peeled down her lacy
panties. She scrutinized her reflection critically. Her
full breasts, slender waist and long legs attracted men's
lust. Her near-purple eyes, curly dark hair and creamy
complexion further complicated the problem. Men
were quick to tally up her physical assets and assume
that if she were given a brain scan, any variation from
a straight line would be purely accidental. Men frequently refused to look beyond her appearance and
considered her to be just another mindless beauty.

"They're wrong," she said, turning away from the
mirror and going into the bathroom to run water into
the tub. "I'm more than flesh and bone."

She'd been blessed with a sharp, inquisitive mind
and a keen interest in medicine. Lack of funds had
prevented her from applying for medical school, and
because her sister's hospital expenses had depleted her
parents' savings, she'd put herself through nurse's
training.

The Cleos of the world might be perfectly content
wrapping men around their little fingers, but not
Halley. With a certainty born from experience, Halley knew Cleo would have thoroughly distrusted her.
Cleo would have kept one eye on Mark, and the other
eye on her. Women who traded on their beauty zeal-

ously guarded their acquisitions, and Cleo would definitely have considered Mark a valuable acquisition.

Following the same line of thought, she wondered why Cleo had divorced Mark. Or had it been the other way around? Had Mark divorced Cleo and if so, why? If Martha's character analysis of Cleo was correct, she should have clung to Mark tooth and nail.

A low groan of appreciation passed through her lips as Halley eased herself into the hot water. She wiggled her toes and closed her eyes. "A long, hot bath is just what the doctor prescribed," she murmured, sinking low in the tub and feeling her muscles begin to relax.

Halley tried to clear her mind of troublesome thoughts. Reaching for the soap and washcloth, she tried to concentrate on how wonderful the warm water felt, but comments Martha had made insidiously crept back into her thoughts.

"Their marriage fell apart before their first anniversary" particularly annoyed Halley.

Where was Mark's tenacity, his stubbornness? she wondered. He'd certainly been tenacious when he'd blamed her for Jason's problems at the hospital. Halley had difficulty imagining Mark giving up easily on anything—especially a marriage.

She stopped herself from speculating on the reasons for Mark's divorce. She'd look like a waterlogged prune before she could even list all the reasons people decided to obtain divorce decrees. Also, she was honest enough to admit that Martha had prejudiced her in Mark's favor. Martha thought Mark was wonderful and Cleo was a witch. Objectivity was impossible.

"Don't blame Martha for your being subjective," she muttered, tossing the washcloth aside and lathering her hands. "You don't want to find fault with Mark either!"

She made quick work of bathing rather than think any more about Mark. Dr. Abraham was dominating altogether too many of her thoughts. What she needed to do now was be thankful she'd corrected his misguided impression of her and make certain they worked together in a constructive manner. Clinging to that decision, she rose from the tub, stepped on the bath mat, then vigorously rubbed her wet skin with a fluffy towel.

Halley was in bed, curled on her side with her knees drawn to her chest, when the phone rang.

"Twain residence," she answered.

Mark twisted the phone cord around his index finger. His mouth felt dry. He suddenly found his valid reason for calling her at this late hour nothing more than a lame excuse. Telling her about Mighty Joe could wait until morning.

"Twain residence," Halley repeated and then paused. "Twain residence," she said, louder. She could hear someone breathing on the other end of the line and began to wonder if this was an obscene phone call. Her heart pounded. Gathering her wits, she blustered, "No, Fred, darling. It isn't the *precinct* calling. Go back to sleep."

"Who the hell is Fred?" Mark demanded, finally forcing himself to speak. Women! Like Cleo, Halley must change bed partners as often as she changed her sheets!

"Mark? Is that you?"

"Sorry I bothered your lover's sleep," he snarled sarcastically, wanting to physically remove any man who shared her bed. "I'll talk to you tomorrow at the hospital."

"Don't you dare hang up, Mark Abraham." Her ploy to rid herself of a heavy breather had backfired. Despite herself she had to smile. "Fred could be my dog."

"A *police* dog?"

"No. The apartment manager won't even allow a lap dog!" She waited for a response, but Mark was silent. "C'mon, Mark, what's a woman supposed to say when she answers the phone in the middle of the night and hears someone panting in her ear?"

Reluctantly, Mark grinned. He folded his arm beneath his pillow and leaned back against the headboard of his bed. "I didn't realize I was breathing hard."

"Nurses have keen hearing." She snuggled deeper under the covers, pleased that he was no longer snarling at her.

"Mmm. And I didn't realize how late it was either. Did I get you out of bed?"

"Nope."

"Interrupt the late movie on television?"

"Nope."

Her soft, lazy chuckle unleashed his imagination. Where was she? He hadn't woken her. She wasn't watching television. Could she possibly be in the bathroom? Did she have a phone by the bathtub? He shut his eyes, picturing her chin-deep in fragrant bubbles. Heat pulsed through him, teasing him, making him ache.

"What were you doing when the phone rang?" he wanted to ask, but didn't.

"I have a phone next to the bed," she said, wondering why he'd called.

Mark swallowed. "I shouldn't have called."

"Why not?"

"You need your sleep."

Need? Halley repeated silently. Who knew more than a doctor or nurse about human needs? A textbook condensed human needs down to water, food and sex, in that order. Sleep ranked a lowly fourth place. But listening to Mark's voice completely rearranged her priority list. What she needed from him was far more refined than sex.

Halley sighed in frustration. "We agreed to be friends. Friends, like doctors, are always available."

Was that a deep sigh or stifled yawn? Mark wondered. Before he heard the unmistakable sound of snoring, he'd better tell her why he'd called.

"I rummaged around in my attic and found one of Oscar's pals. Do you think Tony will object to my substituting Mighty Joe for Oscar?"

"No, sir." Halley couldn't say the same for the direction their conversation had taken. His abrupt switches from the personal to the professional were maddening. Earlier, when she'd sat on his lap bawling about Jason's treachery, he'd done the same thing. His sole concern had been about Jason's effect on the medical community! Exasperated, she'd resorted to passive aggression. "Yes, sir" and "No, sir" would be the extent of her replies.

"You don't sound too enthused about Mighty Joe," Mark commented, mulling over her formal politeness. "Tony can keep Mighty Joe at the hospital day and night."

"Yes, sir." Halley pressed her lips together to keep from praising him for his generosity.

Annoyed at himself for seeking her praise, he said, "I'll see you at the hospital," when he wanted to draw out their conversation for the sheer pleasure of listening to her voice.

"Yes, sir. Good night."

Halley restrained herself from slamming the phone down and quietly disconnected the line. Of course, that wasn't as satisfying as banging it down, or screaming, or kicking her feet between the sheets. Passive aggression might be more mature, but was far less enjoyable.

Chapter Seven

Mighty Joe has got to go," Jill muttered under her breath to Halley. "He's stealing the show from Oscar."

"Leave them alone," Halley whispered. "Mark knows what he's doing."

Halley settled back on the sofa behind the semicircle of chairs where the children sat giggling and making wisecracks. Oscar and Mighty Joe were the finale to the entertainment scheduled. Her eyes sparkled as she looked around for problems.

Mighty Joe, dressed in a miniature uniform of a marine general, was giving orders to a flustered, disheveled Oscar. In one day Mark had taught Tony the rudiments of manipulating the dummy. The fine art of throwing his voice while keeping his lips closed would be mastered later. For now, Tony concentrated on entertaining his fellow patients by letting Mighty Joe give outlandish orders.

Jill groaned. "Mighty Joe must be a direct descendant of Attila the Hun and Genghis Khan. He's a tyrant!"

"Shh!"

"Don't shush me." Jill covered the side of her mouth with her hand and whispered, "Did you hear what he said? He's ordered the patients' parents to spend equal time in the hospital so they'll know what solitary confinement is like."

Halley caught Tony's eye, grinned and winked her approval. "It's all in good fun. Stop worrying."

"Stop worrying? It's going be too late to worry soon. We'll have a full-scale insurrection on our hands. He just told Dr. Oscar every patient would be issued a syringe kit! Each time we fire a shot, they're going to return fire!"

"Shh! I can't hear." Halley's laughter joined the others. She noticed Mr. and Mrs. Miller practically rolling in the aisle. Laughter was Mother Nature's best tonic. "You have to admit," she whispered, "Tony has been a model patient since Mighty Joe arrived."

"Humph! Last night, he ordered Daniel to sit down and take the load off his feet, then proceeded to tell him roll call was at seven in the morning. Mighty Joe expects punctuality from his troops. Daniel nearly croaked!"

Halley gave Jill a sly smile. "I saw you giving Daniel mouth-to-mouth resuscitation in the lounge."

"Shhh!" Jill completely covered her lips.

"What's that hissing noise coming from the back row?" Mighty Joe demanded. "Do we have a leaky nurse? Get the scalpel, Dr. Oscar. We may have to operate.''

Few were exempt from Tony's humor. He indiscriminately poked fun at the hospital rules, parents, nurses and doctors. Only the young patients were sacred territory.

Heavy coughing from Sue, a patient suffering from chronic asthma, brought Halley to her feet. Silently, half crouching, she moved toward the front of the group. Not now, she prayed. As though someone up above heard her, Sue's coughing stopped.

"You okay?" Halley whispered, kneeling beside Sue's wheelchair.

Sue nodded. "I swallowed the wrong way...went down my windpipe."

"Do you need anything?"

Shaking her blond pigtails, Sue turned her attention toward the dummies.

"Hey! Nurse!" Dr. Oscar called, his voice raspy, sexy. "I need something."

"Something for his throat," the general suggested. "Doctor's get a frog to put in their throats when they graduate from medical school." Tony made the dummy's neck stretch as he cleared his throat and perfectly imitated the sound they'd all heard doctors make.

"Come here and sit on Dr. Abraham's lap. I'll give you a free medical examination," Dr. Oscar offered, his oversize eyelashes fluttering as fast as hummingbird wings.

The kids howled with laughter. They'd been examined. They'd experienced being probed and poked.

The idea of seeing one of their nurses go through the ritual tickled their funny bones.

"No, thanks," Halley said, refusing to step into the limelight.

In the past twenty-four hours she'd struggled to maintain a professional distance from Mark. Sitting on his knee would stir up emotions she had to keep under tight control.

Tony saved her, making Mighty Joe say, "You're a kids' doctor. Keep your stethoscope to yourself." But then Mighty Joe added, "Come sit on Tony's knee. A military man knows how to appreciate a gorgeous nurse."

"Sorry," Halley declined, "I'm on duty."

Chuckling, Tony made Mighty Joe lean toward Oscar. "She respects me. You get no respect. Know why?"

"Why?"

"'Cause military officers smell like Brut and doctors smell like pine-scented spray cleaner!"

The kids' giggles gave Halley a chance to return to her seat inconspicuously.

"Nurse Twain smells like flowers," Oscar countered. "Pine trees and flowers go together."

"You going with her?" Tony asked, forgetting to move Joe's mouth. "I saw a ring on her finger yesterday."

Oscar nodded, bragging, "It's a purple diamond."

"Purple diamond?" Joe scoffed. "Where'd you get it? Out of a bubble gum machine? No wonder she isn't wearing it today. I'd give her *real* diamonds."

"You give her trouble!"

"You've got a smart mouth for a dummy," Tony bantered.

"I can sing. Can you?"

That was Halley's cue. Oscar and Joe would sing with the patients, and afterward treats would be served. Martha would keep her eyes on the patients while she and Jill put the last-minute touches on the banquet table.

At lunchtime the children had been served the traditional Thanksgiving turkey and dressing from the hospital kitchen. Dinner was a special treat: hamburgers, fries and milk shakes, donated by McDonald's. The dietitian had arranged for a special sugarless milk shake for Judy.

Hopefully, Halley mused, the food and the entertainment will ward off the holiday blues.

"I think we're ready," Jill said in a low tone. She swept her blond hair back from her face.

"Do you have any plans for this evening?" Halley asked, suddenly realizing how lonely she was going to be once their shift was over.

Jill grinned. "Yeah, I've got a date."

"Anybody I know?"

"Daniel."

"Oh."

"That was certainly a benign 'oh.' You aren't still mad at him, are you?"

"No, but . . ."

"Halley, I know Daniel. He didn't mean anything by it. His making a pass is as harmless as another doctor shaking your hand."

"But . . ." Halley started to warn Jill about Daniel's being in the hospital with liquor on his breath, but decided against it. Jill wasn't a fledgling nurse straight out of school. She was experienced enough to know what she was getting herself into without any friendly advice from her. "Be careful."

Jill laughed. "Too late. Oh-oh, here they come!"

The kids squealed with delight when they saw what they were having for dinner. This was one meal they wouldn't shove around on their plates.

Martha organized them into a haphazard line. Within a few short minutes the table was nearly empty and the children were seated, happily devouring their hamburgers.

Halley angled her way over to Martha. "Want to go halves on a gallon of spumoni ice cream after work?"

"Thanks, but I can't," Martha replied, keeping a watchful eye out for spills. "I have to pick up my son, Christopher, at the airport. Care to ride along?"

"I appreciate the offer, but I don't want to intrude."

"Don't be silly. I told you I wanted you to meet him."

Halley felt the hair on her neck rise. She turned her head just as Mark stepped between them and asked, "Who are you tricking Halley into meeting this time? Forget matching her up with Dr. Oscar. He's retired for the evening."

Nudging Mark in the ribs, Martha retorted, "You suit Halley better than Christopher. Are you busy tonight?"

"Wait a minute, Martha," Halley protested, her cheeks coloring brightly. "You offered to let me ride along with you to the airport."

"I forgot how much luggage my boy has." She pushed her glasses into place, irritated by Halley's reluctance to be with Mark. She turned to Mark. "Well?"

Mark turned to Halley and echoed Martha's exact tone. "Well?"

Can't the man speak for himself? Halley wondered with annoyance. *First Oscar, now Martha!*

"You'll excuse me, won't you?" Martha interrupted. "Judy is eyeing Sue's milk shake."

Warily Halley glanced up at Mark. His dark eyes danced merrily as he looked at Martha and the kids. Then his gaze returned to her. "Martha can't obligate you," she said.

"No, she can't," Mark readily agreed.

His smile was making her heart beat double time. "I wouldn't want to impose on any plans you have for this evening."

"I wouldn't let you. My plans revolve around you."

"What kind of plans?" The sinking sensation in her stomach made her wonder if she was climbing to the top of a slender limb. Watching him closely, she thought she saw a glint of Oscar's mischief-making sparkle in his dark eyes. She almost expected to hear Oscar's high-pitched voice, but instead she heard Mark's normal baritone.

He leaned closer, whispering, "Nefarious plans. Interested?"

"You mean wicked? Disgraceful?" she queried, to clarify his intentions.

"Hmm," he said mysteriously. "Many years ago what I have in mind was punishable by law. Today, it's perfectly acceptable."

"That covers everything from political intrigue to medical experimentation," she quipped. Mark gave her a sexy look through lowered lashes, making a shudder of yearning slice through Halley. Yes, what he had in mind was definitely illegal back then.

"And here I thought we'd become friends." Mark shook his head sorrowfully. "Friends trust each other."

"Don't pull that on me," Halley warned, wondering what he wanted her to do. "You know the old saying about curiosity and *alley* cats. I've used up enough of my nine lives to be cautious. Besides, I hate mysteries."

"Women love surprises," he countered with a rakish grin. "What I have in mind does include a cloak and dagger."

That smile, the one she'd been desperately craving, turned her knees to water. It made her want to go anywhere, do anything, be it illegal, unethical or immoral! How could a mere smile make rational thought disappear? In his present amicable mood, Mark seemed almost desirable enough to make her forget every lesson she'd learned about men.

She clenched her jaw, her hands, to keep them under control. Her impetuous lips wanted to kiss him. Her fingers wanted to trace the taut bow of his lower lip.

No. She had to hide her weakness to avoid being exploited. One charming smile wouldn't unglue her common sense. "Stop beating around the huckleberry bush and give me a straight answer. What are you planning?"

Mark raked his knuckles across her tight jawline. "Magic."

"I've heard that promise, Doctor," she groaned. "Oscar's blunt chant of 'I want you' is a bit more honest, don't you think?"

Tossing his head back, Mark laughed, drawing Tony's attention to them.

"Hey, Dr. Abraham, did you ask her yet?" Tony shouted.

"I'm trying to," Mark replied.

Her jaw dropped. Quickly recovering, she snapped, "Does this magic have something to do with you and Tony and me?"

"As a matter of fact, it does. While I was teaching Tony, I mentioned practicing magic tricks for the Christmas party. Because of your size, Tony suggested asking you to assist in the Hindu basket trick."

"Sorcery and witchcraft. That's what you meant!"

"Partially," Mark conceded, eyes crinkling at the corners.

He opened his mouth to elaborate, then closed it as Tony wheeled up beside them.

"Are you gonna do it?" Tony quizzed.

Halley quickly looked from Tony to Mark. Both man and boy clearly expressed wistfulness, excitement and anticipation. Who could refuse such a combination? Halley couldn't.

"I'll do it with one stipulation, Tony Miller."

"Here it comes," Tony groaned dramatically. His chin sank to his chest. "I should've had Mighty Joe order her to assist us! Go ahead. Give me my restrictions."

Halley bent, crooking her finger to raise his chin. Fully aware that Tony expected a long list of don'ts, she altered a negative approach to a positive approach.

"I'll help you and Dr. Abraham be *guest* magicians at the Christmas show."

Tony frowned, thinking about the significance of being a guest. "That's all? You aren't going to tell me I can't do this and can't do that?"

"Nope. You're responsible for getting well and staying well."

"No problem." Tony beamed with confidence. "Mighty Joe and Oscar made a few new rules for me. I'm willing to follow the rules of the corps."

Mark surveyed the interaction between Tony and Halley, trying to maintain his clinical detachment while a warm glow spread inside him. What seemed like a lifetime ago, he'd told Martha that he doubted Halley's nursing ability. He'd been wrong about her; she'd been right about herself. She was a good nurse; she had simply made a lousy choice of men.

Considering himself less than a prize specimen of manhood, he scowled ferociously. His chances with Halley were as remote as a snowball's chances in hell. In a moment of weakness she'd kissed him, and days later had cried on his shoulder. Only an imbecile would misconstrue budding friendship for love. There was a world of difference between purple glass and precious diamonds, he mused, disheartened. Neither he nor Halley wanted a cheap imitation of love.

Halley caught a glimpse of Mark's forbidding glare. She'd said something wrong to Tony. Cringing, she wondered if she'd clumsily flicked a raw nerve. Unlike Pete's case, she'd had time to read Tony's medical history and had spoken at length with Mrs. Miller. How had she fouled up?

Tony gave each of them a mock salute and wheeled away, anxious to tell the others about his upcoming participation in the Christmas program.

"How'd I mess up this time?" Halley demanded, chin thrust forward aggressively.

Her question jerked Mark from his introspection. "You handled Tony perfectly."

His unexpected praise astonished her. "Then why the frown?"

Mark shrugged. "I was thinking about something else."

"Murder? It's illegal," she retorted in an attempt to inject some humor into their conversation. Her gibe failed miserably. Mark's hard look remained menacing. Halley begun to babble nervously, "I'd appreciate a ride home. Snow flurries are predicted. Between today being a holiday and the weather forecast, I'm certain the buses will be running off schedule."

"You don't have any business standing on the street corner after dark waiting for a bus. I'll meet you at the side entrance that leads to the covered garage."

Considering herself temporarily dismissed, Halley nodded. Shoulders stiff, she strode toward the banquet table where Martha and Jill stood. She'd seen their furtive glances. Since she'd asked both of them what they were doing after work, she knew they were speculating about the conversation between Mark and herself.

Martha cut right to the heart of the matter as Halley came within speaking distance. "Did Mark ask you for a date?"

"No." Martha's crestfallen face matched Halley's own response. Fortunately, she'd been able to disguise her disappointment—she hoped. "Tony cooked up the idea of my assisting them with a few magical tricks for the Christmas program."

"A foot in his door is better than a kick in the pants," Martha said, sounding profound.

Halley cocked her head, uncertain she'd heard Martha correctly. "Sage advice from your nineteen-year-old?"

"I read that in an insurance salesman's office," Martha replied, grinning. "I'm not certain I know what it means either."

"Whatever it means, I have a simple message—go get 'em, Halley. You're the only nurse he's shown the slightest interest in," Jill said and glanced at her watch. "Isn't it about time to herd the patients into their rooms? The doctors will start rounds soon."

The next hour was routine but hectic. Halley performed her duties with meticulous precision, but it wasn't easy. Her stomach was aflutter in an acute anxiety attack.

Within minutes Mark would be striding down the corridor toward her. She repeatedly reminded herself that she didn't have reason to be nervous. She had only asked for a ride. It wasn't as though she roped and hog-tied him, demanding he escort her home.

No, but Martha had figuratively twisted his arm.

Somehow Halley couldn't imagine Mark Abraham doing anything he didn't want to do. Martha was formidable, but Mark was obstinate. Well, it was too late to worry about why he agreed. She had to concern herself with what to do once they arrived at her home.

Should she invite him inside and offer him a cup of coffee? Would that appear overly friendly—pushy, forward? Heaven forbid! She might have convinced him of her innocence regarding Jason, but one smile didn't mean he was going to allow her into his private life.

She did have Martha to thank for telling her about Mark's ex-wife. Cleo had probably chased him, maybe even seduced him. Halley grimaced. As shy and backward as Mark was, seduction was a necessity. Otherwise, he'd...

Halley broke off her thoughts. In two seconds flat she'd gone from drinks to seduction. What in the world had come over her?

"You don't need a man," she whispered to herself, practicing her standard litany. "You don't need a man."

Her loud whisper echoed in the empty corridor. Glancing around to make certain no one had heard her, she realized that she could shout it until her lungs hurt, but it wasn't wholly true. She huddled into the corner by the exit.

No, she didn't need men, in general, but what about one particular man? What about Dr. Mark Abraham?

"I don't need him, either," she staunchly denied.

Liar!

"I don't!"

Liar!

Halley lost the argument. Lying to herself just didn't work.

So? What are you going to do? Cleo seduced him. Can you?

"No," she replied. Her eyes squeezed shut, she burrowed her nose into the velvet lapels of her tweed coat, and dug her hands deep into her pockets. She felt the purple glass ring. Without realizing what she was doing, she rubbed the stone.

"I wish..." Her eyes opened as she slid the ring on her fourth finger. Her lips curved at her foolishness. Wishing on a fake purple diamond was ludicrous. Next thing she knew she'd be out scouring the antique shops searching for Aladdin's lamp.

Halley chuckled. She was too practical, too rational to believe in magic rings. They didn't exist in today's world.

"Sorry I'm late," Mark called from down the corridor. "Rounds took longer than I expected. Ready for a little magic?"

"Ready."

Unavoidably, she brushed against his coat front as she passed through the door he held open. Their eyes met, but they quickly glanced away. Halley hastened her steps to match his gait.

"Brr!" Mark wrapped his arm around her, drawing her close to his camel hair coat to protect her from the biting wind. "The hospital would have had an ice sculpture out front if you'd waited for the bus."

"Too cold for snow flurries." Puffs of crystallized moisture accented each word. Mark curved his body to block hers from the gusts of wind blowing between the hospital and the garage. It wasn't necessary. The temperature could have been below zero and it wouldn't have affected her.

The mad dash between buildings was invigorating, or so she told herself. She avoided the thought that being in Mark's embrace heightened the color in her cheeks more than the cold air did.

Inside the six-story garage the wind howled through the empty spaces. They hurried to the doctors' reserved parking spaces. Mark directed her to the passenger side of a sleek, silver Mercedes. He unlocked and opened the door.

Halley shivered as she sank into the plush leather seat. She cupped her hands and blew into them.

"Sorry I didn't have time to warm the car up." He started the engine, glancing at Halley, noticing she wore no gloves, no scarf and no woolen hat. Lord, the woman needs a keeper! He removed his leather glove and took her hand, lacing her fingers through his. Lightly he tugged her hand until she moved across the seat closer to him. "Stick the other one in your pocket. My car warms up fast once it gets rolling."

Obediently Halley stuck her hand in her right pocket. He put her other hand above his knee while he backed the car from the parking space. Her fingers should have been cold, but weren't. They tingled. Before she had gathered her wits enough to remove her hand, Mark covered it with his.

"Better?"

Speechless, Halley nodded.

"Moist air off the Gulf is moving up the Mississippi valley. Guess that's why we're in for a snowfall by morning."

Halley mentally shook herself out of the stupor caused by touching him. Surely she could carry on a mundane conversation about the weather. "Any accumulation expected?"

"Nothing significant. Kansas City is in for a rough night. But you know the old saying about St. Louis weather—if you don't like it, stick around five minutes and it will change. Erroneous weather forecasting is the rule, not the exception." Mark told himself that he was stroking the back of her hand only to keep it warm until the heater came on.

"The bus schedules are really a mess when it snows. Thank goodness I'm off duty tomorrow." Her eyes strayed from where his thumb lazily stroked hers to the street. "We're going the wrong way. I live . . ."

Mark looked at her questioningly. "I thought we agreed to work on the magician's act."

"Tonight? Now?" So much for inviting him in for coffee. She was going to his place. For better or worse, he'd eliminated her choice.

"Why not? You don't have anything planned for this evening and neither do I. Why delay the inevitable?"

Halley swallowed. The inevitable? A tiny thrill ran through her.

"Christmas is just around the corner," Mark continued persuasively, but he wondered exactly whom he was trying to convince with his sales pitch—Halley or himself. "Magic tricks take a while to perfect. There's nothing worse than bungling in front of an audience."

His thigh muscle flexed under her hand and she loosened her hold. Don't panic, she warned herself.

What's wrong with two friends spending Thanksgiving evening together, working on a Christmas program?

Who do I think I'm kidding? Halley thought. If we go to his place we're going to do more than work on magic tricks.

Who do I think I'm kidding? Mark asked himself. My invitation is about as transparent as they come.

Mark caught Halley's surreptitious glance.

She knows.

He knows! she realized as soon as their eyes met.

Hot air smacked them in the face as the heater came on full force. Mark disengaged his hand from hers. "Do you mind?"

"N-n-no," she stuttered, unable to stand the thought of his putting more distance between them.

She'd fought his charisma. She'd withdrawn when she'd wanted to draw closer. She'd tried to keep her thoughts on a platonic level, but it hadn't worked. A wry grin twisted her mouth. *Play for him; tonic for me,* she mused, remembering Jason's words.

She could dither from now to kingdom come, but one fact was unavoidable: she was falling in love with him.

She'd drifted into a relationship with Jason. He'd skillfully pulled every string tied to her heart to get into her apartment, and later her bed. Sex between them had begun as curiosity on her part and physical release on his. Love had never entered the picture. Mutual satisfaction hadn't either. He'd accused her of being cold, and she'd believed him.

Would the outcome be the same with Mark?

No, she told herself. Mark was different. From the beginning he'd pulled the rug from under her feet. Predictably, she'd fallen—hard and fast. There wasn't any comparison between the men or their effect on her.

In a roundabout way, Mark had been bluntly honest with her by having Oscar tell her precisely what he wanted. Before he kissed her, he'd made his motivation perfectly clear. He wanted sex with no entanglements, no promises, no impossible dreams, and no purple diamonds.

Touching the stone, she made her decision. She wasn't a coy virgin. Unlike Cleo, she wasn't trading sizzling sex for a wedding ring. She respected Mark's integrity. She wouldn't play the seduction game.

Mustering her courage she blurted, "Mark, can I spend the night with you?"

Chapter Eight

Stunned by her unexpected request, Mark unintentionally depressed the gas pedal as he swerved into his driveway. Halley slammed against his side. Instantly realizing his mistake, he braced his arm in front of her while he slammed his foot on the brake to avoid plowing into the garage door.

The car stalled.

As though the mechanical failure wasn't enough punishment for his ulterior motives in bringing her home, the ache of desire he felt for her made coherent speech difficult. Touching the soft fullness of her breasts with his forearm only intensified his masculine need.

"I should say, no, you can't." He draped both arms over the steering wheel and rested his forehead against the backs of his hands. "Damn it, Halley, I planned on tricking you into my bedroom."

"You did?" His confession should have made her angry, but it didn't. A feeling of pleasure flowed through her.

"Yes! All those vague hints I threw at you had nothing to do with magic. I needed a civilized excuse to get you here." His head rocked back and forth on his hands. "I schemed and plotted, practiced what I'd say to you, how I'd act. Lord, woman, I could have discovered a cure for the common cold with the energy I spent thinking about you. Put plain and simple, you're driving me crazy."

Halley reached for him. Her hand trembled, hesitated, then wove its way through the soft short hair at his temple. He raised his head and his dark eyes blazed with fiery light as they turned toward her.

"Pity?" he asked, uncertain of what he saw in her eyes.

"That's the farthest thing from my mind," Halley responded candidly. Her fingers traced the faint line over his brows. "While you were planning my seduction, I was considering seducing you."

Mark twisted toward her. He clutched her slender shoulders. "Seducing me would be easy."

Loving you would be easy, she thought. Her long, tapered fingers splayed from the sensitive spot below his ear across his prominent cheekbones. Could you learn to love me in return? Would Mark find her lacking once they'd made love? Self-doubt, Jason's final legacy, afflicted her.

Her eyes closed as his lips painted fragile kisses across her forehead, her arched brows, her dark lashes. In the cozy warmth of the car, she unbuttoned their coats, shrugging hers off as he shed his, then Mark tossed both coats into the backseat. The necessary delay left both of them shaking with a sense of urgency.

"You're so lovely," Mark said, his large hands caressing her adoringly as his eyes met hers. "So incredibly lovely."

In the blanket of darkness, her eyes shone like diamonds in a velvet sky. She silently begged him to love her, not for the sake of her beauty, but for what she felt inside. She watched his lashes droop, close. Her breath caught. With unerring accuracy, his lips covered hers with a reverence that made her heart pound in anticipation.

The hammering of his heart matched hers. His hands persuasively lingered on her face and hair, coaxing her to acquiescence. Her skin reminded him of porcelain, fine and smooth. Strands of her lush dark hair clung to Mark's fingers as he'd known they would. He'd never seen such loveliness, he thought, uncertain he had any right to touch perfection.

For once, he allowed his heart to rule his head. Who was he to question the gift of benevolent gods? He'd treasure the moments they shared without questioning what the future held. It was enough, for now.

His fingers trembled as they dropped from her hair, to her slender shoulders, on downward. He cupped her breast in his palm. Through the fabric of her blouse his thumb circled the tip, teasing it to erectness.

Halley gasped as a shaft of exquisite pleasure flashed through her. Her immediate response to his touch surprised and delighted her.

Jason had maligned her for not having the good grace to at least fake a response. Could it be that Jason had lied when he accused her of being cold? Had he been covering up his own inadequacy by belittling her?

She abhorred comparing Mark's tender fondling to the way Jason had touched her, but she couldn't stop herself. Jason had grabbed; Mark stroked. Jason had snatched at her clothing; Mark's slow conquest over the small fastening of her blouse inflamed her desire. Jason had hurried their lovemaking; Mark expressed a ferocious need, but it took forever to feel the rough texture of his hand on the creamy smoothness of her flesh.

Fire raced through her from head to foot as his tongue sensuously flicked the corners of her lips. Thoughts of Jason and her lack of ardor with him vanished as Mark claimed her mouth, branding his gentle imprint on her soul.

Her hands slipped to his shoulders. She needed something strong to clasp. She found it as her fingers made quick work of the buttons on his shirt. The sleek skin covering his shoulders cloaked the power of his muscles beneath it. She was safe, secure.

She heard the seat release, felt it push backward as Mark turned her across his lap. Her body fit perfectly against his from shoulder to hip.

He deepened their kiss. His tongue swirled against hers. He tasted sweet and hot. She craved more—more of his passion. His slow exploration became demanding. The silent message his tongue evoked was one of yearning, desire, intense need.

He shifted, pulling her into a snug embrace in which her breasts were pressed against his hard chest. She twisted, loving the feel of his chest hairs against her sensitized skin. His lips trailed from hers until he nibbled her earlobe, sucking her tiny sapphire earring between his lips.

"Mark..." She arched her back, exposing the vulnerable pulse pounding erratically at the base of her neck. Moist kisses stung in a direct path from her pulse point to her nipples. She felt weak, pliant, but still her fingers tugged him closer. It felt good. So good.

Mark heard her whisper his name. The subtle fragrance of her perfume engulfed him in a lush bed of springtime violets. He cupped her breast in one hand, loving its weight, loving how her nipple pearled into a tight bud as his teeth and tongue teased and plucked. As he drew her into the hot moistness of his mouth, her legs pressed against his thigh. His hand ran the length of her leg. His fingers slipped beneath the hem of her skirt.

Her nylons felt cold and silky. Through a haze of passion, he realized how dangerously close he was to stretching out on the seat and sinking into her womanly softness.

"We've got to stop." His fingers disobeyed his own weak command. He nudged her knees apart. Sliding both of them into the plushness of the leather seats, he situated her half beneath him. "We've got to..."

Yes, we do, Halley silently agreed. For a brief moment she considered where they were and what they were about to do. Her eyelids opened for an instant. The windows were fogged from the heat radiating from their entwined bodies. Darkness shrouded them in privacy. She could not voice a protest. She wondered if Mark had the strength of will to stop.

Halley tossed her head from side to side as if to deny the impossible. An abrupt halt would endanger the spontaneity of their passion. Uneasiness would grow between them if they paused, rearranged their clothing and made their way into the house. This special moment would be lost forever.

What she felt didn't require a wide bed and satin sheets. She wanted Mark here and now. Her wantonness might embarrass her later, but she couldn't have cared less. The place they made love was completely unimportant.

Small, purring, incoherent sounds passed between her lips to encourage him. She aided him as he removed her remaining clothing. His fiery skin protected her from winter's cold night air better than a full-length mink.

Mark's boldness and agility would amaze him later. The steering wheel, rearview mirror and lack of space were only mild inconveniences, not obstacles. He adjusted effortlessly to their confinement. He moved Halley and himself with confidence beyond his realm of experience.

Instincts as old as time and as young as new love taught him lessons he'd never learned. Five senses weren't enough though. He savored the feel of his hair-roughened skin against her softness. He absorbed her scent, making it part of his own, making her part of him. He heard the low gasping sounds she made. His dark eyes smoldered brightly as he tasted her sweet essence. And yet, he knew what he felt in his heart surpassed even the intense pleasure bombarding his senses. Passion might lead them to an incredible peak but love would carry them even higher.

He exploded inside of her with a strength that bonded them together for eternity. It left him breathless, exhilarated and exhausted. Never had he felt more like a man, and less than a man. While they were one, omnipotence was his.

A small smile curved Halley's lips as she hugged Mark. She'd learned the truth about herself. Making love with Mark was dying and going to heaven. The passion she'd shared with Mark had invalidated all of Jason's accusations. If she'd been cold sexually, the fundamental problem had been Jason's, not hers.

Mark nuzzled his chin into the hollow of her neck. Slowly he became aware of his weight pressing Halley deep into the leather cushions. "Am I too heavy for you?"

"No," she protested when he braced his arms to move himself. "Not yet. Hold me."

"Sweetheart . . ."

His endearment opened her eyes. Her contented smile widened. "Hmm?"

"Much as I'd like to spend the rest of the night here, the neighbors will be shocked tomorrow morning when they open the door and find two frozen bodies inside the car."

"Lock the door," she teased, kissing the crown of his head.

"Why didn't I think of that simple solution?" His lips grazed the tip of one breast, then playfully nipped the other until it budded between his lips. "I don't have enough energy left to crawl into the house anyway," he confessed amiably.

"Your backside is getting cold." Her hands skimmed his buttocks and flanks. Her sensitive fingertips thoroughly investigated the triangle of dimples low on his spine.

"My front side is plenty warm. In fact, it's hot." Mark lifted his head and gave her a decidedly wicked grin. "Maybe I'm not exhausted. With a little encouragement, I could—"

"Reach across the seat and get our coats?" she hinted lightly. "I just thought of something worse than having the neighbors discover us."

"What?"

"Having an ambulance deliver you to the emergency room for treatment of frostbitten buns."

He grinned, kissing her. "That would be difficult to explain to Martha. I'd never live it down. I vote for letting the neighbors find us."

"Or we could gather up our clothes and make a mad dash for the back door."

Mark's lips lingered on the tilted corner of her mouth. "Or I could press the garage door opener and drive into the garage. It's heated. So's the house."

"Hmm. All the modern conveniences." She was losing interest in anything other than the forays his lips were making beneath her ear. Her hands lazily warmed his backside. "I'm plenty warm."

"Your ears are cold."

"Do something about it," she coaxed.

Mark tapped the tip of her nose in rebuke for her naughty suggestion. "I will. But first, I'm taking you inside."

He braced one hand on the floorboard and the other on the back of the seat. The steering wheel provided him with the balance he needed to make it possible for her to duck under his arm and scoot to the passenger's seat.

Halley put her hand over her mouth, but Mark heard her giggle. He shot her a quelling glare, but a devilish twinkle in his eyes spoiled the effect. Manipulating their bodies into such a twisted position had been easy. Getting back to normal took ingenuity.

"Didn't your mother ever tell you it's not nice to point and giggle?" Mark asked, feeling simultaneously ridiculous and high-spirited.

"Nope. But she did warn me about staying out of the backseat of a '55 Chevrolet. Wonder if she'd object to a Mercedes."

Mark slid into the driver's seat, started the engine and chuckled. "Nobody would believe you. Not even your mother. Not even *my* mother. And she knows I've been practicing magic tricks. For that matter, I'm not quite certain I believe that it's humanly possible for a man my age to make love in the front seat of a car. Crawling in and out of a Hindu basket has to be less difficult."

"Oh, yeah?" she challenged. She draped her arm over his shoulders and rubbed like a kitten against the side of his arm.

As he gunned the motor, the headlights reflected off the garage door, and lit the car's interior. Her firm breast jiggled against his biceps, teasing and provoking him once more. He wrapped his arm around her slender waist and gave her a sound kiss. "Behave," he ordered huskily.

Her fingers wound through the dark hairs of his chest. She twisted several around her finger. "And if I don't?"

Mark pressed the automatic garage door opener and shifted the car into drive. His eyes never left her as it inched forward safely into the confines of the garage. He closed the door, which creaked as it lowered, sealing them in a warm, private cocoon.

"You'll really have something to tell your mother," he promised, cutting the engine. He glanced down at himself, and Halley followed his gaze, smiling when she saw he was once again aroused. "With us, the impossible is probable."

Her hand lowered until her fingers surrounded him. He inhaled sharply, his chest expanding to full capacity. Halley marveled at her power to excite him. She watched his eyes squeeze shut at the immense pleasure she was giving him.

"Oh, sweetheart, you're making me wild." His hand jerked clumsily for the handle to open the door. "We're getting out of here before I pull you on my lap..."

"Sounds like the best idea we've come up with so far," she murmured enticingly. The power he'd given her made her heady. She looped both arms around his neck. One leg gracefully swung over his thighs. Her bare foot touched the heated concrete. Ever so slowly she lowered herself onto him. "Any objections?"

"Welcome home," he whispered, arching upward.

Afterward, Mark carried her to his bed. For long minutes they lay in each other's arms, her head cradled in the the crook of his arm. His heartbeat slowed to a strong, steady pace. Her fingers idly played in the dark hairs on his chest.

Her gaze strayed contentedly around the room. Mark's taste in furniture was a reflection of himself. His matching dresser, armoire and headboard were made of strong, solid woods. Handsome, sturdy, and functional, Halley mused in idle contentment. She had drawn the bedspread willy-nilly across her breasts and over one shoulder and noticed that its collage of geometrical shapes contained the same shades of blue as the pinch-pleated draperies that covered the wide windows.

She glanced at the brass lamp on the nightstand. The telephone beside the lamp was blessedly quiet. She wondered if Mark had called his answering service to let them know he was at home.

A small box caught her eye and held it. Mark had admitted to plotting ways of getting her into his bed. Realization struck with the force of thunder. He'd been more than prepared for her seduction. He'd been prepared to protect her. His plans had been meticulous in detail, but she had ruined them with her impetuosity.

Silently she blasted herself. Every woman knew the risks involved in madcap lovemaking. Not once, but twice, they'd taken that risk without a thought about the consequences. Figures spun dizzily in her mind as she calculated the time of the month and the risk. Apprehension skittered along her spine making it stiffen.

Spontaneity has a price tag.

Could she be pregnant? Would she have to bear Mark's child alone? Her lips thinned into a taut line. It was too late to do anything about it now. Regret, like hindsight, was of minuscule value in planned parenthood.

Her thoughts turned to the future. Her love for Mark would grow with each passing month, she told herself. He would willingly shoulder his responsibility as father of an unborn child. Her confidence in him left little room for doubt. She wouldn't be alone. He'd take care of her.

Her positive attitude withered when she remembered what Martha had said. Mark's first wife had trapped him into marriage and the marriage fell apart in less than a year. Had Cleo resorted to feminine tricks to capture Mark? Halley's imagination ran wild, comparing her circumstances to Cleo's.

Had Cleo trapped him by telling Mark she was pregnant? Then had she been forced to set him free when he discovered she wasn't?

How could she keep a straight face and tell Mark she hadn't intended to use pregnancy as the bait in a trap? She was a nurse. He'd believe the old wives' tale about storks delivering babies long before she could convince him of her innocence. She couldn't even convince herself!

Halley tried to calm down and tell herself she was getting upset for no reason. After all, the odds were with her.

Doctors' offices were filled with women who did everything from taking their temperature daily to charting their most fertile time of the month. They didn't get pregnant. She could be worrying about nothing.

Stop it! Next you'll convince yourself that Mark is madly in love with you.

Halley refused to indulge in self-deception. She'd face the music if need be. One thing was for certain, she'd been stupidly lax, but regardless of tonight's consequences, she wasn't going to trap any man into marrying her.

Mark stilled her restless hand. "Do you have something against hair on a man's chest or do you like bald men?"

"Sorry." Halley hid her concern behind a smile. "I was wondering if you'd called your answering service."

"I'll hear the beeper." Instinct told him something else was bothering her. "You aren't having second thoughts about staying here, are you?"

"No." *It's too late for second thoughts. Life didn't come with an instant replay button.*

"What's wrong then?"

"Nothing's wrong." Feeling uncomfortably close to confiding her speculations, she glanced around the room searching for a safe topic of conversation. "Is that Oscar's trunk?"

Mark stifled a yawn. "Yes, but I temporarily stored him in the nurses' lounge. Oscar enjoys the view." Sleepy though he was, he noticed Halley's effort to be modest. Enticing mounds and valleys with buried treasures lay beneath the fluffy confines of the bedspread.

"Three in the front seat of the car would have been crowded." She chuckled at the thought of Oscar's raging over being tossed into the back seat with the coats.

"Oscar insists on being buckled in for protection against my crummy driving," Mark joked. He noticed that she glanced toward the nightstand after he'd said the word "protection." His eyes followed the same path. *What a blockhead,* he thought. "Halley, I should have protected you."

Her refusal to look at him led him to guess that she'd hastily calculated the risk. "What are the chances of your getting pregnant?"

"Don't worry about it."

Mark curved his finger under her jaw and forced her to face him. "What does that mean? Of course I'll worry."

"You aren't responsible for my actions," she replied.

"What?" His hand dropped to her shoulder and clasped it. He wanted to shake any silly nonsense regarding her taking full responsibility right out of her head. "You make it sound as though you threw me down on the front seat of the car and had your way with me." He snorted at the ludicrous idea. "In case you didn't notice—I wasn't shouting rape."

Halley heard a muffled sound coming from the winged back chair in the corner of the bedroom. "Your beeper is paging you."

Flipping the covers to the foot of the bed, Mark jumped from the bed. "Don't think for a minute that we've finished discussing this," he warned, reaching for the phone. "We haven't."

They had finished as far as Halley was concerned. Certain his answering service would beep him on Thanksgiving Day only in a case of dire emergency, she pushed the covers back. Mark rolled backward and caught her arm. They both knew she could strug-

loose from his light hold, but the message in his eyes compelled her to remain on the bed.

"Dr. Abraham. What's the problem?" Mark listened, but kept one eye trained on Halley. "He what?"

She watched him cover the receiver with his hand, heard him mutter an expletive that Halley felt certain was foreign to his daily vocabulary.

"I'll be there in ten minutes. Call the hospital and tell them I'm on my way. They're to keep Tony as quiet as possible."

He released his grip on her wrist as she asked, "What's going on?"

"Tony is raising hell. Daniel left orders for Mighty Joe to be removed from his room after he fell asleep."

"Why?"

"Who knows? Tony woke up and has threatened to tear the hospital apart." Mark hastily began to dress. "You understand that I have to go, don't you?"

"Of course you do, but Tony is Daniel Edwards's patient. Did they call him first?"

"He's supposed to be on twenty-four-hour call." He hiked up his pants and zipped them, shoving his bare feet into his shoes at the same time. "His answering service has been trying to reach him for more than an hour. He doesn't answer the beeper or his home phone."

"He's with Jill."

"Do you know where?"

Halley shook her head. "Jill didn't say."

She had her suspicions though—the nearest bar. Celebrating a holiday provided Daniel with a socially legitimate excuse to drink. The chief of staff might

give Daniel a slap on the wrist for being unobtaina-
ble, but Daniel would be in serious trouble if he arrived at the hospital while inebriated.

"I can make an educated guess," Mark grumbled,
silently condemning Daniel for being the worst skirt-
chaser on staff. "I've got to cover for him." He
dropped a quick kiss on her forehead. His eyes lingered on her love-swollen lips. Lines formed between
his hairline and eyebrows. Duty calls, he reminded
himself sternly. He shrugged his arms into the sleeves
of his overcoat. At the bedroom door he wheeled
around. "Will you wait for me, sweetheart? Please."

Halley nodded, unable to refuse him anything,
charmed by his affectionate term.

Mark flashed her a grateful smile. "I'll be back as
soon as I can."

She jumped from the bed and ran to the window
when she heard the door leading to the garage slam
shut. She parted the drapes, shielding herself by
slanting the fabric in front of her.

Snowflakes the size of quarters drifted from a pitch-
black sky. Halley shivered. The winter storm must
have bypassed Kansas City. St. Louis was in for a
rough night weather-wise. Slick streets would hamper
Mark's journey to the hospital. She gauged the depth
of accumulation based on previous snowstorms. Two,
maybe three inches had fallen. At the present rate, by
midnight there would be six or seven inches on the
ground.

Twin beams of light backed down the steep driveway. Uncertain that he could see her, but wanting to
prolong their parting, Halley put her hand against the
windowpane.

Mark glanced upward. Although he couldn't clearly see her features, the sight of her hand pressed against the window tugged at his heartstrings. Her simple gesture reminded him of a puppy he'd once seen in a pet shop with its nose making prints on the window. It had seemed to be saying, "Don't leave me. Take me with you."

He blinked the headlights and saw her wave goodbye. In a moment of weakness, he wished she would beckon him to return. He wanted to stay, but had to leave. He hoped she understood.

He swore silently as the rear wheels lost traction. He'd be pushing his luck to make it to the hospital. The trip home would pit his determination and driving skills against Mother Nature's handiwork.

He concentrated on maneuvering his car into the street. Where were the snowplows? he wondered. He'd be stuck at the hospital for the night unless the snow-clearing equipment kept ahead of the storm.

Mark seldom begrudged having to return to the hospital. If anything, he hated going home to an empty, lonely house. Tonight he wanted to stay home and couldn't. He actually resented the demands his professional life made on his personal life.

"One of life's little ironic twists," he commented to himself using Oscar's voice.

He turned onto Forest Park Boulevard. Traffic was stopped. Two jackknifed trailers blocked the lanes. Mark quickly deduced that the accident must have happened scant minutes ago. No police cars or ambulances were at the scene.

He glanced over his shoulder. His silver Mercedes was sandwiched between a pickup truck and a low-

slung sports car. He couldn't move forward or backward and he couldn't turn around. Several drivers
trudged toward the crippled trucks; others were returning to their vehicles to wait for the trailers to be
moved.

Early in his career Mark had decided to respond to
roadside emergencies. With good reason, other medical professionals ignored them. Too many doctors
and nurses had found themselves faced with million-
dollar lawsuits to take the risk. Mark had weighed the
cost of his insurance coverage against his ethics. Victims of accidents won hands down.

Mark opened his door and shouted at a man who
was retreating into his car. "Hey! Anybody injured?"

"No. Just a fender bender." The stranger dusted the
snow from his hair. "What a way to spend Thanksgiving, huh?"

"Yeah."

Mark assessed the traffic snarl. Oncoming traffic
was also blocked. If he could get his car across the
median, he'd be able to take the back streets to the
hospital. If that failed, he could desert his car and
walk the remaining blocks. "Hey, Mister, I'm a doctor
responding to an emergency call from the hospital.
Could you help me push my car over the median?"

The stranger nodded, then ducked his head into his
car. The back doors opened and three burly men in
military uniform climbed out.

Mark glanced at his watch. Forty minutes had
passed since he'd received the call. Tony's patience
would be stretched to the breaking point by the time

he got there. The skeleton medical staff would have their hands full if he decided to go on a rampage.

"Thanks, fellas," Mark said, wading through the snowdrift at the inside curb. A couple of other motorists stopped to lend a helping hand. He pointed to the empty lanes across the median. "Do you think we can get it over there?"

"No sweat, man. The marines have landed. We'll get it on the other side of the boulevard if we have to carry it, right, guys?" one of uniformed men replied, jostling the man next to him with his elbow. "Doc, you get behind the wheel and steer. Jack, get the bags of sand out of the trunk, would ya?"

Within minutes the front wheels were over the curb, but the back wheels were spinning in vain. Mark's car rocked back and forth as the men grunted and heaved. "Come on," Mark muttered. "Grab hold."

As though the car had been waiting for his verbal command, it lurched forward. While he fought for control on the icy street, Mark heard the men who'd helped cheering wildly.

"Thanks!" he yelled through the open window. In the rearview mirror, he caught a shadowed glimpse of them waving.

Mark raised the window, leaned forward and concentrated on the treacherous road. The snow fell faster, heavier. The side street he turned onto was lined with snow-covered parked vehicles. He could barely see ten feet ahead of the front bumper.

Hot air from the window defrosters blew in his face, drying the moisture in his eyes. He blinked, clenching the steering wheel with dogged determination. Inside his gloves, his hands perspired.

At the first sight of the hospital Mark began to breathe easier. Two more blocks, he thought, calculating the distance to his destination. Cautiously he inched through the next intersection, ignoring the stop sign.

His hopes of making a return trip home dwindled as the car plowed through a snowdrift. The closer he came to St. Michael's Hospital, the more he berated Daniel Edwards's stupidity. Hard as he tried, he couldn't justify the order to remove Mighty Joe from Tony's room. Selfishness and spite on Daniel's part had motivated the removal. Uncharitable thoughts of what he'd say to Daniel made his scowl deepen.

Mark parked the car in a tow-away zone behind the hospital. Snow swirled around his pant legs as he hurried toward the rear entrance. A loud popping noise from overhead alerted him to the danger of broken power lines. He ran, slipping and sliding, into the hushed safety of the hospital corridor.

His lungs ached from breathing frigid air through his mouth. He forced himself to inhale through his nose as he leaned against the wall and kicked off his galoshes while unbuttoning his coat. Adrenaline pumped through his body, urging him back into action.

Barefoot, he raced to the elevator, his coat flapping at his sides. The stainless-steel door parted the moment he touched the button. His stomach lurched in rebellion against the quick ascending motion.

Mark knew that panic spread faster than a flu epidemic. One patient could upset the entire floor within minutes. Once the children were awake, all hell would break loose. Curiosity was a big factor. The children wanted to know what was causing a commotion. Having witnessed Tony's confrontation with Martha, he knew the boy was capable of causing total upheaval.

Snow clinging to his dark hair began to melt. Rivulets of icy water tracked down his cheeks, but Mark didn't notice. His entire attention was focused on the numbers lighting up overhead.

The doors opened, and Mark charged out. He halted, stunned. A feather could have knocked him over. Silence greeted him. He'd expected to see the night nurses frantically rushing between the nurses' station to various rooms. The red lights mounted over each patient's door were unlit. He strode to Tony's room and found the lights off and Tony fast asleep.

"Dr. Abraham?" a hushed voice called.

Mark pivoted. Cassie Blake, the night nurse, motioned him to the nurses' station.

"What happened?" he demanded, wiping the back of his gloves across his face.

"Didn't your answering service reach you? Just a few minutes after Tony started raising hell, I remembered seeing Oscar in the nurses' lounge." She gave Mark a conspiratorial grin. "Dr. Edwards ordered Mighty Joe removed, but he didn't say anything about Oscar."

Mark hunched over the counter. "End of crisis?"

Cassie nodded. "End of crisis."

"Did the answering service reach Dr. Edwards?"

"Yeah, but they couldn't make heads or tails out of what he was saying." Her voice lowered to a whisper. "Word is, he was juiced to the gills."

"Drunk?"

Cassie shrugged. "I guess so. I didn't talk to him myself. The girl on the answering service talked to Jane, who told..."

Mark held up his hands to stop her. "I'm certain with each telling everyone elaborated on the original story." Remembering how Halley had suffered because of lies told about her, he refused to listen to a fellow doctor being maligned. "Gossip cuts deeper than a scalpel. Let's call a halt to it right here. Okay?"

Cassie sniffed. "Sorry, doctor."

His curtness had offended her. She expected an apology, Mark realized. But she wouldn't get it. He'd made the mistake of listening to Jason Malone lie about Halley. He'd never again listen to anyone make mincemeat of another person's reputation.

"I'll be in the lounge making a phone call."

Chapter Nine

Seven, eight, nine. Halley stared at the telephone silently counting the rings. Shortly after Mark had left the phone had rung six times, then quit. She'd refrained from answering it. She wasn't in her home; it wasn't her phone. Anyone trying to reach Mark at this time of the night had to be affiliated with the hospital. By answering the phone, she'd be letting others know about their private relationship.

She pulled the covers over her head to muffle the persistent tones.

"Why isn't he back?" she muttered, irritated by the caller's persistence.

The weather detained him.

He didn't want to return.

Tony needed him.

He didn't need you.

The roads are bad. He can't return.

A man in love would walk chin deep in snow to return to his lover.

He lives too far from the hospital to wade through the snow.

He'd find a way if he cared—really cared.

He could have been in an accident.

He's lying injured beside the road.

Halley imagined him being wheeled into the emergency room of St. Michael's on a stretcher. In the past, she'd witnessed many such arrivals of accident victims, but the thought of Mark being injured terrified her. She drew her knees to her chest, forming a tight ball of misery. Her mind raced as she tried to remember the names of the nurses who were most likely to be on duty in emergency. The inexperienced nurse that replaced me would be one of them, she decided, gnawing on her bottom lip. I should be there saving his life. She shivered, knowing she'd never forgive herself if something had happened to Mark.

What was she doing lying in his toasty-warm bed while he was at the hospital injured, perhaps dying?

Halley pulled a tight rein on her imagination. Working herself up into hysteria was useless. She had to take positive steps to discover what was delaying Mark.

She could call the hospital anonymously and ask if any car accident victims had been brought to the emergency room. That made sense.

But how could she? The phone was still ringing off the hook.

"Stop ringing!" Halley covered her ears, hoping to block her thoughts and the sound of the phone. "I'm not going to answer it!"

When the phone abruptly stopped, she sighed, peeking from under the covers. Her hand snaked from under the blankets and grabbed the receiver. There was no dial tone.

"Hello?" Halley squeaked, raising her voice an octave to disguise her normal speaking voice.

"Why don't you answer the phone? I must have let it ring twenty times. I thought something had happened to you."

Halley collapsed against the pillow when she recognized Mark's voice.

"I'm fine. I was worried about you."

Her concern dissipated his anger. "It took forever for me to get here. What little traffic there is isn't moving."

"How's Tony?"

"Sound asleep." He relayed what Cassie had done without mentioning the rumor about Daniel Edwards. "Dr. Oscar restored peace and tranquillity before I arrived."

Halley was glad the pediatric ward hadn't been upset by Dr. Edwards's insensitivity. "Did Daniel's answering service get hold of him?"

Mark paused. He trusted Halley to keep her mouth shut, but repeating an unfounded rumor was distasteful. "Yeah. He couldn't get to the hospital."

"Jill lives in North County. The weather is usually worse there."

"Umm," Mark replied noncommittally. "Looks like I'm stuck here for the duration. The radio announcer says that the police department has shut down the main arteries in the city until the snow equipment clears the interstate highways."

"How long will it take for them to remove the snow from Minneapolis to St. Louis?" Halley asked in a teasing tone.

Mark chuckled. "Forever!"

She felt the same way. His double bed seemed twice as large, and three times as empty as hers at home.

"Are you in bed?" he asked, picturing her with her dark curly hair spread on his pillow.

"Yes."

Mark cleared his throat as if to remove the rush of desire that threatened to strangle him.

"Wish you were here?" she inquired provocatively.

His affirmative reply hissed across the ice-coated telephone lines. "There has to be a bright side to this situation, but I sure can't find it."

Halley grinned. "Tony's okay. That's good news."

"Yeah." Mark stretched out on the sectional sofa in the lounge and crossed his feet at his ankles. He'd accepted the fact that he couldn't be with her. He'd have to make do with keeping her on the line as long as possible.

"And you're safely on the pediatric floor instead of lying in the emergency room the way I imagined."

Her being anxious on his behalf pleased him. "I was scared to death that something had happened to you when you didn't answer the phone."

"I was protecting your reputation, Doctor."

"Speaking of protection—we have some unfinished business to talk about."

"Are you alone?" She blushed at the thought of someone overhearing their intimate conversation.

Mark glanced toward the door leading to the nurses' station. Cassie could be eavesdropping. He doubted she would, but wasn't absolutely certain. Recalling how miffed Cassie had been when he cut her short, he decided to delay their discussion.

"No one is in the lounge but me."

"Look over the soda pop machine," she instructed softly. "See that hot air duct? Do you know where it leads?"

"Point well taken. We'll *temporarily* postpone this conversation. It's gone, but not forgotten. Don't get any funny ideas in that independent little head of yours," he warned, hesitant to let the subject drop. "I'm not some callow youth out sowing wild oats."

"Yes, Doctor," Halley replied primly. "Whatever you say, Doctor."

"Did I ever tell you that you have a smart mouth?"

Halley grinned. "You must have my mouth confused with Oscar's. Mine is the one that's smear-proof. Remember?"

"Sweetheart, I remember. With you there and me here, I'm trying my level best to forget!"

Static on the line threatened to make hearing each other impossible.

"Halley?"

"I'm still here, but you're beginning to sound as though we're a million miles apart."

Mark raised his voice. "I'll be right behind the snowplows."

They were disconnected before Halley could reply. She nestled the phone back on its cradle. Grinning, she pulled Mark's pillow to her chest and closed her eyes.

Hours later, she was awakened by the bed shifting under Mark's weight. Drowsily, she rolled to her side. Her eyes opened. Thin rays of sunlight slanted through the narrow opening in the drapes.

"Go back to sleep," Mark whispered. "It's barely dawn."

"C'mere." She reached for him, needing to be held. His skin felt cold. "You're freezing."

"I had to shovel the driveway to get the car up the hill."

Halley fitted herself against his backside and wrapped one arm around his waist. Mark didn't budge an inch. Although half-asleep, her instincts told her something was dreadfully wrong.

"Mark, are you okay?"

"Yeah. Go back to sleep."

His back was rigid, unyielding. His breathing sounded unnatural. She propped herself up on her elbow. He'd pulled the blanket up so far that his face was partially covered. He was shutting her out. She had to find out why.

"Are you sorry I stayed?"

"Don't be silly."

Silly? Frightened, yes. Silly, no.

"Mark, you're scaring me." She scooted to the side and rolled him onto his back. "For heaven's sake, tell me what's wrong."

He kept his eyes tightly shut. Moisture had gathered beside the bridge of his nose. His lips barely moved as he said, "Jimmy Owens is in intensive care."

Halley knew what the transfer meant. Jimmy's tenuous hold on life was slipping. His kidneys were failing.

"Any word on a suitable donor?"

"No."

Halley wrapped her arms around him in compassion. Her soft cheek raked against the dark stubble on his chin. "I'm sorry, Mark."

"Me, too."

She heard the resignation in his voice. His arm slowly stole across her shoulders. His fingers fiddled with a lock of hair at her nape.

"Is there anything I can do?" Halley knew there wasn't, but she felt compelled to ask.

"No."

Mark held back his tears. One of his patients was about to die, and there wasn't anything he could do about it. He'd provided medicines and painkillers, but those were only temporary measures. He'd consulted with the kidney specialist on innovative means to prolong Jimmy's life, but day by day, the little boy had grown weaker. Each time he'd gone into Jimmy's room he'd seen the child's hopes fading. There must have been something else he could have tried. Some treatment he wasn't familiar with that could give them a little more time to find a donor.

"Don't blame yourself. You're doing everything you can," Halley said, knowing she could give Mark only empty words of consolation. She wiped away the lone tear that slid toward his ear. Mark wasn't the type of man to accept a medical failure easily. He cared. His caring hurt him. Trite phrases wouldn't ease his pain.

"I should have left my troubles at the hospital. Cleo always said I had more scars than my patients."

Halley kept quiet. Mark needed to talk and she'd listen regardless of how hearing him speak of his ex-wife bothered her.

"She said I'd get hunchbacked from the weight of carrying the medical world on my shoulders." He inhaled deeply. Exhaustion slowly began to take its toll. His voice became slurred; his sentences became fragments of thoughts. "Said other doctors lead normal lives. Belong to the country club, go golfing, attend social functions, have families. Said I was too busy being superdoctor. Superdoctor," he repeated harshly. He yawned. "Can't even keep Jimmy alive. Failed him...her...everybody."

His arm fell limply on the bed. She raised her head, watching his lips move in his sleep. She couldn't be certain, but she thought she heard him murmur, "Beautiful, so beautiful."

Halley rolled to the far side of the bed and wept for him. Her heart ached with tenderness. He wasn't a failure. Few men had his strength and compassion. Daily he earned every ounce of admiration and respect others bestowed on him. Everyone looked up to him, and yet, he looked down on himself.

Jimmy Owens wasn't the first, nor would he be the last patient at St. Michael's who might die. Mark's optimism and determination to save Jimmy had kept the child going for weeks. The little boy knew Dr. Abraham would do everything humanly possible to make him well. Why couldn't Mark accept his limitations?

Why hadn't Cleo been able to accept them? While Mark had been tearing himself apart over his patients, she'd been in his home shredding what was left of him by making unrealistic demands. Country club activities, Halley thought angrily. Mark should have known that Cleo wasn't the only doctor's wife who begrudged the long hours demanded by the medical profession. Divorce wasn't uncommon among physicians.

So what if Cleo was beautiful? Physical beauty and a marriage license didn't give her the right to belittle Mark.

She scrubbed the tears off her cheeks. She was mad, mad at everyone who'd chipped away at Mark's self-esteem.

No wonder he scowls, she thought. It's his way of keeping everyone, including myself, at a distance. She fervently hoped the smiles she'd seen and the laughter she'd heard were symbols of trust. She wouldn't hurt him. In fact, she'd make certain she protected him from anyone else who dared to nip at his heels.

Too restless to sleep, she eased off the bed. After leaning over and pulling the blankets over Mark's chest, she tiptoed to the closet. Mark's maroon velour robe hung from a hook on the door. Keeping an eye on him, she silently slipped into it. With the stealth of a cat burglar, she crept from the room.

Walking quietly down the carpeted steps, she rolled up the robe's sleeves and knotted the belt. The clean fragrance of soap and expensive cologne clung to the lush fabric. An image of Mark wearing his robe after taking a shower and shaving made her pause to hug herself.

Sunlight reflected off the ice outside, casting rainbow colors through the oval lead glass of the front door. She rushed down the remaining steps eager to view Mother Nature's handiwork.

"Fantastic," she whispered reverently. Her bright eyes sparkled with merriment.

The snow reminded her of happy times in the Twain household. She could almost hear her brother shout, "Gottcha!" as he playfully threw a snowball at her. She remembered the thrill of accomplishment when they'd built a towering snowman, decorated it and pulled their parents from the warm confines of the house to see it.

Snow meant wild sleigh rides down steep hills, followed by steaming hot chocolate. Halley licked her lips. She could almost taste the fat marshmallow floating on top.

Good times, she thought, turning toward the kitchen. She wondered if Mark had similar childhood memories. She pictured him as a small boy bundled from head to toe, tossing his head back, squealing with laughter. Had he built snow forts to hide behind as he bombarded his family with snowballs? Had he been uninhibited enough to sink into the snow, swishing his arms and legs sideways to make snow angels? Was Oscar simply another version of the scamp Mark had been as a child?

Halley genuinely hoped so. She turned, wrapped her arms around herself, giving herself a tight squeeze. The urge to open the door, scoop up a handful of snow, fly back up the stairs and throw it at Mark was tempered only by the knowledge that he had been at the hospital a full twenty-four hours. He needed uninterrupted rest. Later in the day, she promised, with a vixenish smile lighting up her face.

"Yesterday was Thanksgiving. Today is Abraham's Day," she proclaimed.

But first, she'd have to make certain she'd free him from his responsibilities. Mark would waste the day worrying unless he felt certain his patients were well attended.

She strode purposefully toward the kitchen. Glancing around the immaculate room, she saw the telephone on the counter near the dinette table. She dialed the hospital number and asked for Martha Chaney.

"Good morning, Martha," she greeted when she heard her friend's voice. "How's everything in pediatrics this morning?"

"Fair. The kids are excited about the snow. It's your day off. Why are you calling?"

Martha's straight-to-the-point approach eliminated unnecessary chitchat. "I need a special favor."

"Christmas Eve, Christmas Day, New Year's Eve, take your pick. You worked on Thanksgiving."

Halley grinned. "I'll work all three of those days if you'll have someone cover for Mark's early rounds."

"Hmm."

"Is that the sound of wheels turning in your head?"

"Nope. It's the noise I make before I get ready to dispense some motherly advice."

"I took your advice yesterday. That's why I'm here at Mark's house."

"In-ter-est-ing. Care to tell me what are you doing there?"

Halley couldn't resist piquing Martha's curiosity. "Talking to you."

Martha faked a yawn. "Boring." She pushed her glasses up the bridge of her nose. "I can think of better things to do and I'm more than fifty. What's wrong with you?"

"Nothing. Mark spent the night at the hospital. He's sleeping."

"I'll have another doctor take rounds for him. Want a couple of suggestions as to what you should be doing?"

"Nope, but before I hang up, how is Jimmy Owens?"

"He's still in intensive care," Martha said with a sigh. "But he's stable. The kidney specialist has left and says Jimmy's condition won't worsen in the next few days, but what happens after that is anybody's guess."

"Thanks, Martha. See you Sunday. If there's any change with Jimmy call Mark. He'll want to know."

Having accomplished her first act geared toward protecting Mark, she walked to the refrigerator and opened it. One egg, a nearly empty carton of milk, half a jar of orange marmalade and a small package of something that looked like a cross between dried meat and hairy cheese were the only items she found.

The thought of braving the snow in an unfamiliar car while searching for a grocery store had little appeal. Her spirits drooped at the prospects until she opened the freezer compartment.

"Voilà!" She mentally took back every mean word she'd ever spoken about frozen food being the mainstay of a single person's menu. They could hibernate for weeks without leaving his house.

Within minutes she had coffee brewing and bread in the toaster. Mark would sleep for hours. She'd see to it. In the meantime, she'd roam around his home enjoying her freedom to investigate the nooks and crannies of the turn-of-the century mansion.

Halley grinned, shaking her head, and wondering if Mark would think her a snoop. She wasn't exactly. She was simply trying to fit her man into his environment. Her man, she mused. Possessive little dickens, aren't you?

The timer on the toaster oven rang.

"Shh!"

She cocked her head, listening for noise from upstairs. Snow insulated the house from street noise. Warm air passing through the heating ducts and perking coffee wouldn't awaken Mark.

Halley softly hummed a popular ballad as she poured a cup of coffee, placed her toast on a dish and strolled to the dinette table. Seating herself in one of the swivel chairs, she realized how happy she felt. She propped her elbows on the table, lifted her cup and sipped the fragrant brew.

Today would be wonderful. She could feel it in her bones.

Mark reached for Halley. His arm stretched until the tips of his fingers curled around the edge of the mattress. Eyes opening, he glanced at the hollow in the pillow next to his to reassure himself that he hadn't been dreaming.

"Halley?"

He swept the blankets aside and sat up. For the life of him, he couldn't remember anything from the previous night after he'd returned home. She had waited for him, he recalled as he pushed an unruly lock of hair from his face.

"Halley?" To his ears his voice cracked as loudly as a bolt of lightning, while in actuality it was barely above a whisper.

He blinked the sleepiness from his eyes, then glanced at his wristwatch. Noon. He sprang into action. Grabbing his still-damp slacks, he hopped from one foot to the other as he tugged them on. Myriad thoughts cluttered his mind. Had she gone home? There weren't any buses for blocks. Where were his shoes? He'd missed morning calls at the hospital. No appointments today at the office. Why hadn't Halley wakened him to take her home?

Half-decently attired, he charged from the bedroom, taking the steps two at a time. His voice boomed, "Halley!"

She'd heard a scuffling noise from overhead. Sounds as if he's wrestling a baboon, she thought, putting down the book of stage magic she'd been reading and crossing toward the arched doorway that led into the foyer. Lord have mercy! Was he somersaulting down the steps? The front door banged against the wall.

"Halley, you promised you'd wait!" Mark bellowed. Momentarily blinded by the sunshine on the snow, he shielded his eyes with his hand.

"I'm here," she said, standing two paces behind him.

Startled, he spun around, confronting her. His stunned expression was followed by a slow, steady blush that climbed from his chin, over his mouth, up to his high cheekbones. His lips moved, but nothing came out.

"Why don't you shut the door before we both freeze?" she suggested mildly, smiling from the pleasure of knowing his first thought upon awakening had been to find her.

"I—I thought you'd gone home," Mark stammered, shutting the door and shivering.

"Obviously I haven't. Care for a cup of coffee?" She turned toward the kitchen, crooking her finger in silent invitation.

Mark sagged back against the door. The icy glass pressing against his bare back erased any lingering sleepiness. He jolted upright.

The sight of Halley's trim hips swaying gently within the confines of his robe sent hot flashes along his nerve endings. She hadn't gone. She'd waited. A bubble of infinite joy burst, spreading millions of effervescent bubbles through his bloodstream.

He trailed after her. "You should have woken me up."

"Uh-uh." She gestured toward the dinette chair. "You were too pooped to pop, much less..."

His arms circling her waist halted her chatter. Her fingers stilled in midair, then covered his strong forearm. Her head drooped backward to his shoulder and his lips covered the pulse beating erratically at the base of her slender throat.

"Much less?" he prompted huskily.

"Bother with me," she replied, having difficulty keeping her mind on anything other than the delicious feeling his lips created.

"I like bothering with you."

"That's not what I meant." His hand slipping into the gaping robe stole her breath away and made coherent thought impossible.

"Grandma called what I'm doing 'pestering' a woman." He brushed his lips over hers. She tasted of coffee and orange marmalade. "Wanna be the object of some serious pestering after I get back from morning rounds?"

"You missed them." She twisted in his arms and reached around his neck. "I called Martha. Someone else took them, and don't worry about Jimmy Owens. He's stable. If there's any change you'll be the first to know."

"Efficient, aren't you?"

"Hmm." She ran her lips over the whiskers on his chin. "You need a shave."

"Among other things."

"Like coffee and toast? Or would you rather have lunch?"

He nibbled her ear, blowing softly. His palms followed the curve of her spine until they rested on her hips. Feet spread apart, he pulled her closer. "I'd rather pester you."

Halley squirmed against him. "Uh-uh, not yet. I've made big plans for you today."

Rocking her against his pelvis, he let body language speak for him.

"I'm going to tell you exactly what you told me last night—behave." She tried to wiggle out of his arms. "First, you're going to eat a hearty meal. Then, we're going to . . ."

Mark pulled her hips even more tightly against his. "Nurse Twain, haven't you learned that you can't boss a doctor around? Especially when said doctor has you in his amorous clutches?'' Despite his mock scowl and stern tone, a devilish light had kindled in his eyes.

"Oh yeah?" She flashed him a cheeky grin. "Oscar lets you manipulate him into doing what you want. Your patients have to take your orders. Occasionally, as a nurse, I let you dictate to me. But not here. Haven't you heard that a kitchen is a woman's place? You're on my turf."

He chuckled at the way she twisted the phrase, "A woman's place is in the kitchen," to serve the purpose of a liberated woman. Much as he wanted to assert his male dominance he loosened his hold.

"I gather you've made plans for your day off?"

She nodded curtly.

"Do they include me?"

"Most definitely."

Mark grinned. "Do these plans include a bit of diligent pestering?"

"Shame on you," she scolded, taking advantage of his light grip and twisting out of his arms. Halley tightened the belt on the robe, tying an extra knot. She smiled wickedly at him. "Yeah, after a liberal dosage of anticipation, I'm going to pester the life out of you."

He planted a kiss on her forehead, then chortled. "I'm going to fire my receptionist and let you schedule my days. What's first on the agenda?"

"You shave and shower while I fix something for you to eat."

"I don't suppose . . ."

"No. I'm not going to scrub your back," she stated staunchly. Putting words in his mouth for a change felt great. She turned him toward the door. "I spent the past couple of hours reading your magician's manual. Poof! Vanish!"

"I'm gone. I expect applause when I reappear though," he said. He winked at her sexily, then whistled "Anticipation" as he bounded from the kitchen and up the stairs.

One thing about frozen food in a plastic pouch, Halley thought as she opened the bag containing chicken à la king, it's fast. Deftly she spooned the mixture over toast points.

She mentally timed how long it had been since the sound of water running in the shower had stopped. The heaping plates were on the table when she heard Mark coming down the steps.

Putting her thumb and index finger beneath her tongue, she blew an earsplitting wolf whistle as he entered the room. "Better than mere applause?"

Mark nodded. "I've always wanted someone to teach me how to do that. Who taught you?"

As she lowered her fingers, her eyes widened appreciatively. Clean-shaven, dressed in a pair of navy wool slacks, with a cherry-red ski sweater covering a white shirt open at the throat, Mark looked like a new man. She knew she was staring, but the dramatic change had the same effect as being tackled and having the wind knocked out of her. His eyes seemed to smile at her in amusement.

"Halley?"

"Uh, yeah, lunch is ready."

He snapped his fingers in front of her eyes, then pointed to his mouth. "Who taught you to whistle?"

"Oh! My brother." Feeling a trifle weak-kneed and dizzy, she sank into the chair he held for her. Her stomach fluttered. Could it be morning sickness already? Impossible!

"In the busy schedule you have planned, do you think you could spare a few minutes to teach me how?"

"Yeah. It's a simple matter of holding your mouth right." Her starry eyes clung to his lips. It was little comfort to Halley that the silly smile on his face was an exact replica of the one on hers.

Pretending to smooth the paper towel on her lap, Halley ducked her head. His special brand of charisma could only be taken in small doses. Much more and she'd overdose.

"Lunch looks great," Mark complimented, aware of the blush tinging her cheeks. Had she read the X-rated thoughts he was struggling to hide? Knowing the only thing between him and his heart's desire was his robe was having a disastrous effect on him.

"Mr. Stouffer, Mrs. Swanson and I are old friends. They prepare most of my meals," she said.

Picking up his fork, Mark pushed a chunk of chicken around in the gravy. His libido hadn't responded to a cold dousing in the shower. He wanted her so badly he doubted he'd be able to swallow a bite of food.

"Mine, too." He peered out the window. Icicles hanging from the roof were dripping steadily under the late November sun. "It's stopped snowing."

Her eyes met his for an instant, but she quickly glanced away.

"We could build a snowman," she said, acting as though the pimiento on her fork was utterly fascinating.

"Or go ice skating on the pond in back of the house. My sister's skates are in the basement somewhere."

"That would be fun," Halley agreed, faking a smile. "Do you have a sled down there, too?"

"Yeah, but one runner is broken." Mark cut a toast point with the edge of his fork. "We could take a long walk." *Up the stairs,* he mentally added.

"And have a snowball fight."

Their eyes met and held. Mark grinned. He looked up toward the master bedroom over their head.

Halley put the remains of her twisted napkin on the table. "Or?"

"I could build . . . a fire."

A roaring fire was already building inside Halley. "In the fireplace?"

"Hmm." Mark took her hand, lacing his fingers between hers. "I'd let you skate your fingertips around on my chest."

"We won't have to search through the basement, will we?"

Mark stood, drawing Halley to her feet.

"And I could teach you how to hold your mouth exactly right. . . ." His lips touched hers in a brief but tantalizing kiss. "Hmm. You are a fast learner."

"And in return, I'll teach you the old-fashioned way to pester a man."

Hand in hand, touching from shoulder to thigh, they moved from the kitchen to the living room.

"And then," Mark added, "if the snow hasn't melted . . ."

Chapter Ten

Jill closed the filing cabinet with a snap of finality that threatened to awaken the sleeping children. Halley glanced from the nursing station down the dimly lit corridor. Less than half an hour ago she'd made rounds. Everything, with the exception of Jill, was calm and serene between the hours of two and four.

"Daniel wasn't plastered," Jill stated unequivocally.

"Only saints are plastered. He's no saint."

Jill groaned and pinched her nose. "Your sense of humor stinks."

"Right along with Daniel's breath."

Halley gave Jill a long level look. Although she feared that Jill was perilously close to tears, Halley resisted the urge to give her any insincere reassurances.

Daniel had arrived late for evening rounds, smelling like the inside of a gin bottle. Twice in one week was inexcusable. He had to be stopped.

"I'm driving him to drink? Is that what you're insinuating?"

"No. With you at his side, he's spending more time with his patients, but even so he's sometimes conducting rounds while half polluted."

"For a nurse who professes to be worldly, you're making noises like a prude. Come on, Halley. Other professionals have a two-martini lunch. Do you think their secretaries go around sniffing their breaths?"

"They would if they were on the receiving end of a medicine bottle. He could overdose a kid, don't you realize that?"

"You're overdramatizing, aren't you? None of his patients are suffering from receiving an incorrect dosage."

"Yet," Halley said. "I've watched you check his patients' charts."

"That's part of my job. His patients receive excellent care."

"What about Tony on Thanksgiving night? Everybody, including Daniel, knows the kid has a short fuse on an explosive temper. If Cassie hadn't been quick on her feet, Tony could have caused a major problem. You were with Daniel. Was he drinking then?"

Jill shrugged dismissively. "He'd had a couple of glasses of wine with dinner. The rumor circulating about him slurring his words is a gross exaggeration."

"Sure it is," Halley replied with a hint of sarcasm belying her words. "Daniel's explanation for ordering Mighty Joe to be taken away from Tony was so garbled that the answering service called Mark. While Daniel was relaxing with a drink in his hand, Mark was struggling through a blizzard. Tony is Daniel's patient, not Mark's.''

Jill leaned over Halley's shoulder and whispered, "How clearly do you speak when you're in the throes of passion? How much sense would you make in similar circumstances?"

"Very little," Halley admitted honestly.

Jill's liaison with Daniel was the worst-kept secret of the decade. Heat from the smoldering glances they'd been passing back and forth was enough to melt test tubes.

Was she jealous of their relationship? Halley wondered. Yes, she admitted finally. She wished Mark would be as demonstrative with her as Daniel had become with Jill.

Inside St. Michael's hallowed halls, Mark acted as though the surgeon general were considering putting a warning label down her back that read: Loving Halley Twain may result in heartache, heartbreak and terminal lovesickness.

Outside the hospital, he was everything a woman in love could ask for. Since the Friday after Thanksgiving, they had spent as much time together as their schedules allowed. Mark rarely smiled in her direction at St. Michael's, but she had heard a rumbling belly laugh when he'd watched her grunt and squirm into the three-foot tall Hindu basket as they'd practiced for the Christmas show. He'd cackled with fiendish wickedness as he pretended to saw her in half. And later, in bed after making love, his peaceful, angelic smile had been enough to sustain her through the work day.

Working the midnight shift was less than ideal for a budding relationship, Halley thought, but . . .

Jill moved closer, shrewdly inspecting Halley's dreamy smile. "What difference does it make to you if Mark had to make a midnight appearance on the pediatric floor? He probably wasn't doing anything important anyway."

The lead in Halley's automatic pencil snapped. Jill's rhetorical question indicated a ready willingness to listen to any hospital gossip about Mark. Schooling her features into a placid mask, Halley nonchalantly twisted the point of her pencil to lower more lead into position.

"Mark's private life isn't being discussed by everyone from his associates right down to the lady who scrubs the floors. Daniel's is."

"Those other doctors are jealous of Daniel's reputation, his good looks. It's envy that's behind this malicious gossip. We both know how petty women can be. Men aren't any different."

"You won't sidetrack me with false justifications," Halley chided. "You're letting your affection for Daniel distort your judgment."

Jill put both hands on her hips and glared at Halley. "Daniel is a fine doctor. Do you realize that he's on staff at two other hospitals? The other two are a lot more prestigious than St. Michael's. Do you think they'd allow drunken behavior? Someone around here has it in for him." She leaned toward Halley until their noses almost bumped. "You don't like him, either, do you?"

"You're sidetracking again." Halley pushed her chair backward. "My personal opinion of Daniel Edwards is unimportant. You're implying that Daniel is running himself ragged between three hospitals, but that doesn't excuse his drinking."

"It's all stress-related. He's overworked. He has to unwind from the pressure. Since when does a cocktail at lunch make a man a drunk? He's human just like the rest of us!"

Halley shook her head. "A two-martini lunch is fine for a businessman. A businessman goes back to the office and shuffles papers until he's sober. Daniel is a doctor. A man whose judgment is impaired by alcohol shouldn't be making life-and-death decisions."

Reasoning with Jill was getting them nowhere, fast. Better to drop the subject while they were still being civil, Halley decided. Their friendship was her reason for initiating the conversation. Halley hated the idea of running to Martha like a tattletail, but Jill was leaving her little choice. To do less would result in Halley's being an accomplice should anything happen.

"What's the news on Jimmy Owens's condition?"

"He's hanging in there." Jill pulled up a chair next to Halley's. "Don't cut me off. Please. I hear what you're saying. You're my friend, but I'm in love with Daniel." Her chin dropped; her hand rubbed her stomach protectively. "I'm the one who popped him in the nose for fooling around with other women after he'd slept with me."

Halley inhaled as though Jill had punched her in the solar plexus. Now she understood why Jill had given Daniel a tongue-lashing when she'd first been introduced and Daniel had come on too strong. Jill had said that "I'm late" was on Daniel's list of most hated expressions. Perhaps, Jill's words had not been just meaningless sarcasm, but had a far deeper meaning.

No wonder Jill had been distressed the day Mark had stormed from the lounge with fire in his eyes. Jill had been angry with Daniel for making a pass, but it hadn't been mere friendship with Halley that had caused her fury.

As the silence grew between Halley and Jill, all the little pieces of previous conversations began to fit together, taking shape, pointing to the reason for Jill's deaf-and-blind posture concerning Daniel Edwards.

"You're protecting Daniel and your baby, aren't you?" She covered Jill's trembling hands. Halley swallowed sympathetic tears. "Think, Jill. Who's going to protect his patients?"

"Me. You. You're my friend. You'll help me, won't you?" Jill's shoulders shook with suppressed sobs. "Please. Between the two of us we can keep him straight."

"Keep him straight or cover up for him?" Halley asked, caught in an untenable situation. Her compassionate nature made her want to help Jill, but at the same time, she had a responsibility to Daniel's patients.

"Nothing criminal, I promise. Halley, I know he's going to propose soon. When he does I'll make certain he gets help if he has a drinking problem."

"Have you told him that you're pregnant?"

Jill shook her head. "I can't."

"Let me think about it, will you?" Halley stood. "I've got to set up the medicine trays."

"I knew I could count on you," Jill whispered. "You're my friend."

As Halley strode from the nurses' station she tried to put herself in Jill's place. What would she do if she caught Mark staggering through the hospital corridors?

Her vivid imagination ran dry. Workaholics and alcoholics don't mix, she mused, grateful that Mark was too big a man to make the same mistakes Daniel had made.

Drawing on her experience with Jason, she knew exactly what she'd do in Jill's place—what she'd done. But her situation had been different from Jill's. She'd never loved Jason. Compassion was a pale substitute for genuine love.

Halley frowned. She pulled a tall stool from under the counter in the medicine room, sat down and stared at the bottles in the cabinet.

Was she letting generosity and compassion make her soft-headed again, this time with Jill, under the guise of friendship?

Had she forgotten the lesson she'd learned from Jason? He'd taken advantage of her, but only because she'd let him. She hadn't been hard-hearted enough to call his bluff, to say, "Go ahead. Do whatever you want to do. I have my own life to lead."

Gut-level, she knew exactly what she should do. First thing in the morning, she should file a written report with Martha Chaney. By nightfall, Daniel Edwards would be called in on the chief of staff's carpet.

Then all hell would break loose. Halley rubbed her forehead, picturing the scenario that would unfold.

Martha would be obliged to pass on the report, but that didn't mean she'd enjoy it. Like most efficient administrators, Martha preferred to have everything running smoothly. By making waves, Halley wouldn't endear herself to the head nurse.

Jill would be a basket case and feel that Halley, her friend, had betrayed her. In her anger and hurt, she'd whisper recriminations to the other nurses. Halley could picture herself entering a room and listening to the whispers turn into stony silence.

And Daniel? He'd be sober as a judge when he denied the allegations. He'd point his finger at Halley and cry, "insubordination" or "incompetent" or something worse.

The mental picture darkened to pitch-black, but she could still see one thing quite clear: packing up, moving on, searching for another job. In the final analysis, Daniel would survive and she'd be sacrificed.

Halley bit her bottom lip. "I'm not a martyr! Joan of Arc didn't wear orthopedic shoes!"

She reached down and rubbed her calves. Although martyrdom lacked appeal, she had to do something. To Halley, keeping silent meant condoning Daniel's behavior.

Her thoughts returned to Mark. She wondered if he knew the reason Daniel had been unable to get back to the hospital Thanksgiving night. Surely he did. Why hadn't he said something to her the next day? Intuitively, she knew the answer: Mark didn't spread rumors. But did he believe them?

He'd believed Jason's lies.

There were moments, even during the past two weeks when they'd been practicing magic tricks, when he'd give her a peculiar look. She'd also caught his furtive glances at her when she was working with his patients. He wanted to trust her—he did trust her—but there was still some unresolved element of doubt in his mind.

Did Mark have the same doubts about Daniel? Even if he did, suspicions and hard evidence were two different things. She needed proof, but getting it was easier said than done. What could she do, sniff Daniel's breath, then drag him to Mark's office and say, "Here. Take a whiff"?

No, the likelihood of Daniel's tamely allowing her to prove his guilt was slim.

She was right back where she started. Daniel's drinking while on duty was a menace to his patients. Filing a report without substantial proof would only result in Halley's becoming the subject of ridicule and Daniel getting off scot-free. She had to do something, but she'd have to wait for the right opportunity. Going off half-cocked would cause more problems than it solved.

Halley glanced at her watch. *I'll find some way to talk to Mark*, she thought. *He'll believe me.*

Mark's rubber galoshes lost traction in the packed snow. He recovered his balance by grabbing hold of a nearby tree. "Hey! Halley! Over here! What do you think of this one?"

"It's scrawny compared to this one." Halley pointed to a spectacular eight-foot tree. The heels of her boots sank into the ruts other Christmas tree shoppers had made in their quest for the perfect tree. Head tilted back to peruse the top branches, Halley beamed. "This is ab-sol-lute-ly perfect."

Laughing at her imitation of Martha Chaney's way of stretching a multisyllable word when she was excited, Mark slopped through the snow and stood beside Halley.

"Let me turn it around so we can see it from all sides."

He missed seeing Halley's intense expression as he yanked the tree from its stand.

Halley had spun Jill and Daniel's problem round and round in her mind until she was dizzy. She'd planned on having a serious talk with Mark about it, but when he'd picked her up at the hospital, eager as a small kid buying his first Christmas tree, she hadn't had the heart to dampen his enthusiasm.

"Is it too big for your Christmas tree stand?" Halley asked, practical to the very end.

Mark winked sexily, then pounded the trunk on the ground to shake the snow from the boughs. His eyes sparkled with happiness. "No problem. Mine's adjustable. Fits all sizes."

"Oh, yeah?" Halley gave him a playful punch in the ribs to pay him for switching to Oscar's tenor voice. "You're a rascal, Dr. Abraham."

Balancing the tree with one hand he wrapped his arm around Halley and pulled her against him. His lips brushed across hers for a second. "Only with you, sweetheart, only with you."

"Ever made love in a Lion's Club Christmas tree lot?" she quipped, as she nibbled his lower lip.

"Nope. But have you noticed that when you're with me I park my car in the most isolated spot available?"

Halley groaned. "I'll never live that down, will I?"

"It's not something I'm likely to forget." He kissed the tip of her bright red nose. "Oscar's grandkids will love hearing about Great-uncle Mark's first date with Halley Twain, won't they?"

She squirmed closer. "What about *your* grandkids? Are you going to tell them everything you know, you rat fink?"

Mark let go of the tree. It tottered, then slowly fell backward into the snow.

"Are you telling me something I have every right to know?"

"I'm not telling you anything. I was asking."

"Halley." Mark spoke her name in a low menacing voice.

"Yes, Mark?"

"Are you?"

"Am I?" Halley teased, getting even in advance for his threatening to be a blabbermouth.

"Pregnant."

"You know what, Mark? It's so cold tonight that when you exhale and steam comes out of your nose— you give a perfect imitation of a fire-breathing dragon. Maybe..."

"No maybes. Answer my question and quit stalling. Are you or aren't you?"

Halley stepped back and pointed toward the fallen tree. "That's definitely the best tree on the lot. I hope none of the branches split when you let it fall."

Her immediate problem of what to do with Daniel's being intoxicated while at the hospital had first priority tonight. Besides, she couldn't answer Mark's question.

She continued to chatter. "Do you think the Lion's Club has the rule that if you break it, you pay for it? I always hate going into a store when they have that rule. Just as sure as Santa Claus gets stuck in chimneys, I'm the one that breaks something expensive...."

Mark muffled her running monologue with a kiss. "I gather you don't know."

"One time—" Halley shook her head "—I was in a knickknack shop, the one where I bought the swan in my living room, and I was looking at a lead crystal figurine of a unicorn."

"Was that a 'No, I'm not' shake of the head, or an 'I don't know' shake?"

"*I don't know* why I didn't see the plaster of paris giraffe on the floor."

"You will keep me informed, won't you?"

"*Of course*, I didn't know a thing about how fragile plaster of paris can be. I barely nudged it with my toe. The next thing I knew, I was paying for a giraffe."

"I'm going to keep pestering you until I know for certain," Mark warned.

Halley dug her hand between his elbow and his coat. Grinning like a Cheshire cat, she said with hidden meaning, "I'm prepared to be pestered by you. In fact, once we've decorated the tree, I'm going to do some 'pestering' myself."

A surge of warmth claimed Mark. He was the last person in the world to argue with her. He'd break speed records decorating the tree. "See that little bitty one over there?"

Halley tossed her head back and laughed. "No, Mark. We've decided on the tree. Come on, pick it up and let's get going."

An hour later, Mark wrestled the tree into the stand in the center of the living room floor while Halley wrestled with how to bring up the subject of Daniel's problem. Finally as she straightened out strings of tiny clear-colored lights that twinkled like stars, she hit on a way.

"Want me to fix a hot buttered rum?" she offered, knowing Mark planned on dropping in to visit with Tony after he took her to work.

"Can't." Mark stepped back to make certain the tree was straight. "Do you think we'll have enough ornaments?"

"Between the two of us, we should have more than enough. How about some eggnog laced with brandy?"

"No, thanks, but feel free to fix yourself a cup of hot chocolate if you're still cold." Mark nudged aside the box he'd hauled down from the attic. "We'll put your ornaments up first. Mine are all pink and bur-gundy-colored."

Halley tried not to giggle, but she did. She crawled on her hands and knees to the giant-size box where his ornaments were stored. All thoughts of casually bringing up the topic of drinking while on duty fled.

"Pink and burgundy?"

"Yep, Cleo hired her interior decorator to pick them out." He could laugh now, but years ago Mark had silently grimaced when the effeminate decorator had hung a melon-sized ball on a scrawny branch of a flocked artificial tree. "The dark red ones match the leather chairs. Don't ask me what the pink ones match. Probably the decorator's jockey shorts."

Halley's eyes widened as she ripped off the tape and opened the box. "Oh, my!" She picked up one monstrosity, holding it up to the light. Inside the iridescent bubble a tiny ice skater twirled, hands above her miniature head, toes pointed. "This is really something."

"Yeah. Something I should have left in the attic."

Fascinated by the craftsmanship, but repulsed by the ostentatiousness, Halley carefully put it back in the box. "Mine are the six for $1.99 variety. They don't match anything."

Mark grinned, marching over to the boxes he'd carried in earlier. "Do they have sparkle and glitter glued on the sides?"

"You'll probably think they're gaudy." She ignored him, picking up another of Cleo's ornaments. On the inside of this one, she saw tiny silver packages wrapped with miniature silver bows. How in the world had they gotten them in there? she wondered.

"Wow!" Mark dropped to his haunches with his back to her and held up a dark green ball with gold glitter banding the center. "My mom and dad had a whole bunch of these when I was a kid. Do you have any of the sunburst kind that dip in the middle and have a fake stone that shines when you hold it up to the light?"

Halley wasn't listening. She deposited the ornament back in the box, wishing she'd left her conglomeration of decorations at home.

Feeling a bit forlorn, she compared her Christmas decorations with Cleo's. Glitter and glitz versus style and sophistication.

She glanced down at her worn jeans. Cleo had probably worn a shimmering hostess gown while watching the decorator put the final touches on the tree. As Halley plucked at a loose thread in her sweater the yarn began to unravel, leaving a small hole.

What a comedown for Mark.

"We could buy some new ones," she muttered self-consciously as she knotted the woolen thread. "Or just use yours."

"Are you kidding? These are perfect." He opened another box and chortled with glee. "Why didn't you tell me you brought some lights? Look! You've even got the icicle kind."

Halley cocked her head, listening to him in disbelief. "You like them better than these?" She dangled a rope of twinkling miniature stars.

Rolling to his feet, Mark stared at her as though she'd sprouted another head. His smile dazzled her. "Infinitely better."

"Really?"

"Hmm." He dropped down beside her and framed her face with his large hands. "Yours are beautiful. They're real Christmas ornaments for a real Christmas tree. I couldn't be happier."

Halley glowed inwardly. She turned her face and placed a warm kiss on the palms of his hands. His eyes blazed brighter then the stars on the rope of lights.

"I don't suppose you'd consider waiting until later to decorate the tree, would you?" he asked, taking her with him as he lay down on the thick carpet.

"There's still plenty of time before Christmas." Halley licked her lips. They felt parched from the heat of his gaze. "An hour or two of delay won't make any difference."

Mark nodded. His forefinger traced the natural arch of her brow. *She's so incredibly beautiful and so very, very real,* he thought. He searched her brilliant eyes for a special gift that only she could give him. He fervently wanted to hear her say, "I love you."

In the short span of time they'd been together, he'd traveled a million light-years away from the despair Cleo had brought him. Jason's lies and the rumors he'd spread were also buried in the past. They'd come a long way in a short time.

Mark trusted Halley. He was ready to love, to be loved, but was she?

"Halley..."

"Hmm?"

Her fingers followed the uptilted bow of his mouth. His smile belonged to her. She wasn't going to destroy it by bringing up unpleasant things. Tomorrow, she promised herself, yes, tomorrow she'd bring up the subject of Daniel.

"Will you..." He swallowed the marriage proposal on the tip of his tongue. It was too soon. Two pieces of vital information were missing. Did she love him for himself? Would she or wouldn't she want his child? He finished his question with a sigh. "...go to the annual Christmas party with me?"

Chapter Eleven

Tomorrow never comes. Trite, but true, Halley thought, watching Jill follow Daniel into Tony's room.

Several days had come and gone. They were back on the day shift. Jill protected Daniel like a mother hen with a single chick, steadfastly keeping him distant from Halley, making it impossible for her to determine if he'd been drinking.

Martha bumped Halley's arm. "Tonight's the big night. Your dress is hemmed and hanging in the closet in the lounge."

"Thanks, Martha. I owe you another Italian dinner."

"Don't thank me. I'll get all the thanks I need when I watch Mark's blood pressure skyrocket when he sees you struttin' your stuff."

Halley grinned. "Struttin' my stuff?"

"Did I say it wrong?" She removed her glasses and scrubbed them with a disposable tissue. "I swear, keeping pace with Christopher's lingo is a full-time job. You should have seen the look of horror on his face the other night when I referred to his long-haired roommate as a hippie flower child. He says I'm in a sixties time warp, lost aboard the starship *Enterprise*."

"Wearing a mini skirt and dancing to Beatles music, right?"

Martha groaned. "Music—that's another sore subject. For six years, I paid a small fortune to give Christopher private violin lessons. What does he do the minute he sets foot on a college campus? He pawns his violin and buys an electric guitar." She plopped her glasses back in place and rubbed her ear. "I'll be deaf before it's time to ship him back to school."

"Does that mean you won't gripe about not *hearing* from him?" Halley teased affectionately.

"Letters were invented by the mothers of college kids—such a blissfully quiet form of communication. No whang, whang, whang!" Martha glanced toward Tony's room. "The Millers are taking Tony home today. I hate to admit this, but I'll miss having Mighty Joe issuing new hospital regulations. He's made me think twice about some of the standard hospital rules."

"Speaking of rules..."

Martha held up a finger for Halley to wait a second while she answered the muted ring of the phone. "Pediatrics. Nurse Chaney speaking."

Finally, Halley had the perfect opening. Tony was Daniel's patient. Daniel was breaking hospital regulations. She hoped she could ease the direction of their conversation around to Daniel's strange behavior.

"Yes." Martha's blue-gray eyes lit up. "Yes!" she said excitedly. "I'll send him right down."

"Martha? What is it!"

"They've found a donor for Jimmy Owens. The kidney specialist wants Dr. Edwards down there immediately."

"Wait a minute. Jimmy is Mark's patient."

Martha bustled around the counter. "Dr. Edwards is also a consultant on this case. Mark is out of his office on an emergency call and can't be reached."

"But . . ."

Martha dashed down the corridor before Halley could formulate an objection.

Halley had to get hold of Mark. Should one of the doctors be needed to assist in the surgery, she wanted Mark to be available. Lu Anne, Mark's receptionist, would know how to locate him. Her fingers shook as she reached for the phone and dialed the number.

"Dr. Abraham's office."

"Lu Anne? Halley Twain here. Is there any way I can reach Mark?"

"Hi, Halley. He's on an emergency call outside the hospital. Don't worry. He won't be late to pick you up tonight."

"Do you know exactly where he is?"

"No. Is something wrong with one of his patients on your floor?"

"No." Halley couldn't confide in Lu Anne without it seeming as though she was repeating gossip. "Never mind. I'll see if I can locate him."

Just as she put the receiver down, Daniel sped toward the elevator with Jill at his heels. Hushed whispers were punctuated with quick nods. Halley watched Daniel go into the elevator leaving Jill behind with her knuckles pressed to her lips.

"Jill," Halley called softly, controlling her rising panic. Martha was returning to the nurses' station. "Could I speak to you for a moment in the lounge, please?"

Martha heard the request and glanced at the clock on the wall. "It's a bit early for an afternoon break, isn't it?"

"Do you mind watching the desk? This won't take long." Halley saw Martha's perplexed expression, but she couldn't stop to explain. She had to know exactly what Daniel had had to drink with his lunch.

Martha made a shooing motion with her hand. "Go ahead."

Jill preceded her into the lounge.

"I want some short answers and I want them fast. Did Daniel have anything to drink today?"

Keeping her back turned, Jill mumbled, "I don't know."

Halley wheeled Jill around by the shoulders and gave her a sharp shake. "Don't protect him when Jimmy Owens's life could be at stake. One more time, and I want a straight answer. Did Daniel have a drink at lunch?"

"I don't think he did, but I wouldn't swear to it. Halley, I asked him the same question and couldn't get an answer! Don't you think I know what could happen down there?''

Halley felt Jill's shoulders begin to shake. "Could you smell alcohol on his breath?''

"No, but he had a breath mint in his mouth." Tears gathered in her eyes. "He seemed okay. I swear he did.''

"That's exactly what you may have to do—swear it—in a courtroom, under oath," Halley threatened. "Can you?''

"Yes." Halley heard her answer, but Jill was shaking her head from side to side, avoiding eye contact. "Yes, I will.''

"What do you expect me to do if something happens? Do you think I can live with myself knowing I put your friendship ahead of my professional responsibility? I should have confronted Daniel myself.''

"He'd only deny it.''

"Then I should have gone higher." Thanking aloud, Halley said, "I should have reported him. It may not be too late.''

Fear lit Jill's eyes. "Don't, Halley. You're making a terrible mistake. Don't stir up trouble. If you're wrong, you'll be the one everybody hates. You'll be fired.''

But what if I'm right? Jill saves Daniel. But who saves Jimmy?

Armed with those questions, Halley dropped Jill's arms and rushed back to the nurses' desk.

"Martha, I have good reason to believe that Dr. Edwards is under the influence of alcohol." The head nurse's gasp didn't stop Halley. "I could be wrong, but I can't take the chance.''

"She is wrong," came Jill's voice from behind Halley. "I went on afternoon rounds with Daniel. He's stone-cold sober."

Martha looked from Jill to Halley, then to the man stepping from the elevator. "Mark!" She motioned for him to join them while speaking to Jill. "I want you to tell me what you know about this while Halley talks to Mark."

"She's causing trouble." Jill pointed an accusing finger at Halley. "Daniel gave her the brush-off and she's trying to get even by saying he's drinking while on duty."

Raising both hands, Martha shushed Jill. "Halley, it'll be an hour or so until the operation. Daniel Edwards's reputation is at stake. I want these conversations kept between the four of us until . . ."

The fierce scowl on Mark's brow prevented Halley from hearing Martha's final words. She tilted her chin and stiffened her back. Win, lose or draw, she'd gone too far to back down.

Jill's accusation echoed in Mark's head, making him feel as though a knife had been plunged into his flesh.

Insecurities he thought were dead and buried surfaced. What does that make you? he asked himself. Second choice? Third?

Halley swung around when she heard the door shut. "Mark, you can't let Daniel assist with the operation."

Leaning against the door, arms folded against his chest, he marveled over how being upset enhanced her beauty. Cheeks flushed, violet eyes clear, lips parted,

Halley was far more beautiful . . . far more treacherous than Cleo.

"Why?"

"Why! Didn't you hear what Martha said?" Halley paced the length of the conference table. Her hand trailed over the Formica top as though the smooth surface would calm her nerves. "Dr. Edwards could make a serious mistake!"

She looked over her shoulder at Mark. Of all the people on the staff, he was the one she'd counted on to believe her without question. And yet, he was standing there, staring at her skeptically.

"Did you have lunch with Daniel?"

He struggled to keep his voice at a normal pitch. The thought of Halley and Daniel sharing an intimate lunch was illogical. A nurse's schedule provided time for a quick trip to the cafeteria, at best. Usually the nurses brown-bagged their lunch. But his logic had taken a back seat to the jealousy that prompted the inquiry.

"Of course not," Halley snapped.

"You didn't see Daniel have an alcoholic beverage?"

"No." She mimicked his dry tone. "I didn't see Daniel have an alcoholic beverage."

"Then how do you know his judgment is impaired? Did he bounce off the walls as he staggered down the hallway?"

"No!" Mark's sarcasm pierced her confidence.

"Was he loud or boisterous?"

"No."

"Did he reek of liquor?"

Her voice became smaller and smaller. "No."

"Then why are you making this accusation?" *Daniel gave her the brush-off and she's trying to get even,* he repeated to himself. He'd seen Daniel and Halley that time in the lounge. There might have been other times, other places when he hadn't seen them. Had she been two-timing him? Had the love he felt for her blinded him? Had Jill covered for Halley until now?

Halley covered her eyes with her hands. "Mark, I know he's been drinking."

"How do you know? Are you seeing him after hours?"

"You know who I've been with every minute that I haven't been on duty." Her hands dropped limply to her sides. She couldn't look at him, not after that question. *He must think I've been sneaking around here at the hospital,* she deduced.

Her eyes felt dry and scratchy. *This is far worse than I thought it could be. He's the one person I truly thought would believe me without reservations.* Tears finally reached her eyes and her vision blurred.

Mark turned his head away from her. His last question had been demeaning, but he hadn't been able to stop himself from asking it. Daniel loved to relate accounts of his sexual prowess. It was possible...

It's not! his subconscious shouted loudly enough to blare through the jealousy motivating his doubts. *Daniel might; Halley wouldn't!*

"Do you remember the day you came into the lounge and thought you were interrupting a cozy scene?" she demanded, realizing he wanted specific incidents to back up her story. To him, she was a nurse challenging the reputation of a doctor. She was accosting the sacred brotherhood of physicians. He wanted hard facts to substantiate her claim. Blind faith, that was what she'd foolishly expected from Mark. But cold facts were what he wanted.

Mark nodded.

"I smelled liquor on his breath."

"You didn't say anything when you came to my office."

"No, I didn't. You still believed Jason's lies about me. You thought I was some kind of a flighty woman out scavenging around for some doctor to keep me. Didn't you?"

"That's beside the point."

"No, it isn't, but we can't argue about that now. Remember the day Daniel refused to let Tony work with a ventriloquist's dummy? Tony blew his cork. I'd settled Tony down, but Daniel was going to administer tranquilizers. He had booze on his breath then. And what about Thanksgiving? Jill admitted they'd been drinking while Daniel was on call!"

"I'm to believe Jill when she says Daniel was celebrating on Thanksgiving, but I'm *not* to believe what she says today? Didn't you hear her? She said your wild accusation is motivated by his lack of interest in you."

Halley lunged across the room and grabbed his shirt in her fists. "I know you've heard the rumors about his being so drunk the answering service couldn't decipher what he said."

"You want me to believe rumors? Do you want me to believe Jason's stories, also?" he asked sarcastically. "Or do I pick and choose the rumors I believe based purely on what you tell me is the gospel truth?"

Halley saw a mocking smile on his lips. Her palm itched to wipe it off. Mark's fingers dug into her arms.

"Let go of me."

"Let me tell you something I did hear. I heard you asking me if I wanted a hot buttered rum when you knew I was bringing you back to the hospital. What about that, sweetheart?"

His scathing use of the endearment she cherished shattered her control. Her hand flew to the side of his face. She heard the slapping sound and saw the imprint before she realized what she'd done. Her eyes widened.

"Thank you, Nurse Twain." Mark stepped backward, releasing her. He peeled her left hand, finger by finger, off the front of his shirt. "I think you've said everything I want to hear."

"I won't apologize...." Her voice shook; tears threatened to fall. "Never. Not to you. Not to Daniel. Not to Jill."

"Cut the innocent act. Jason called you a barracuda." He raised his hand to his smarting jaw. "Guess I just felt your teeth, didn't I?"

"I'm getting out of here," Halley muttered. Blinded by anger and tears she stormed passed him.

Mark caught her arm. "You'll understand if I'm late picking you up tonight, won't you?"

"Don't touch me, Dr. Abraham." Halley felt as though he'd ripped her heart from her chest. In pain, she retorted, "You and Oscar ought to live together in perfect harmony. You both have eyes that don't see, ears that don't hear...and no heart!"

A facsimile of a smile twisted Mark's lips. "Your exit line is far better than Cleo's. She only called me ugly." He dropped her arm. "Get out, Halley. Get out of my life and stay out."

Halley stumbled from the nurses' lounge. Wordlessly she brushed passed Jill and Martha and headed toward the staircase.

"Halley."

She heard Martha's voice, knew she was cutting her own throat by leaving the floor while still on duty, but she couldn't stop. The scenario she'd imagined had become a nightmare.

Halley was down the steps and outside before she realized where she was. A bus slowed to a stop at the corner. Without a coat or purse, she had little choice. She'd walk, even though she had no place to go.

Mark clamped his hands around the back of a stainless-steel chair beside the table for support. His knees buckled. His stomach twisted, recoiling from her final savage thrust.

Blind, deaf, dumb and heartless. Cleo's parting shot was far kinder, far lest devastating.

His head reeled. He clenched his teeth to keep from bellowing his anguish. The ravaging pain he felt threatened to obliterate him. For long, long moments, he actually felt that he wouldn't survive.

He gulped air into his lungs. Tears stung his eyes. The urge to smash everything around him was tempered by a slender thread of sanity.

He'd handled the situation wrong from the beginning to end. Jealousy and low self-esteem had blinded him from sane reasoning. Jill had planted the seed of doubt. He'd nurtured it, cultivated it...and Halley had harvested it.

A bitter taste coated his tongue. His hands ached from squeezing the metal of the chair. How different this would have been if Jill had kept her mouth shut. Had any nurse other than Halley accused Daniel of drinking, he knew he would have reacted differently. He'd even spoken to the chief of staff himself about doctors resorting to alcohol and illegal drugs to relieve job stress. Granted, he hadn't mentioned Daniel by name, but he'd definitely had Daniel in the back of his mind.

Why'd I do it? he asked. Why'd I push her into a corner?

Because you wanted her to scream, "I love you, Mark." He wanted her to deny Jill's claim, to defend herself by declaring her love for him.

Three simple words would have stopped the demoralizing questions that had begun with, "Did you have lunch with him?"

Had she replied, "No, I love *you*, Mark," the inquisition would have ceased.

But she hadn't. With laser precision his tongue had beamed in on her weaknesses. She hadn't been able to prove Daniel was drinking. Like most capable nurses, she'd let intuition and compassion guide her.

Regardless of Jill's accusation, Mark had to follow his instincts. The patient's welfare came first. The brotherhood of doctors was only as strong as its weakest link. Daniel's role in the surgical procedure would be relatively insignificant, but it could put Jimmy's life in danger. As a doctor, Mark couldn't ignore any element that increased the odds against a patient's full recovery. Like Halley, he cared. Like Halley, he couldn't stand back and do nothing.

Mark picked up the phone and called the extension outside the scrub room.

Within seconds Daniel was on the phone.

Mark gave Daniel a choice: Daniel could willingly withdraw from the Owens case and take a leave of absence to obtain help for his personal problem, or Mark would use every smidgen of his professional clout to have Daniel dismissed from St. Michael's staff and have his license to practice medicine revoked.

Moments that seemed like hours to both men gave Daniel time to consider his options. Knowing he'd finally been caught, knowing subconsciously he'd wanted to be caught, Daniel willingly confessed that he had been drinking and wasn't fit to be in the operating room. Almost gratefully he agreed to take a leave of absence.

Mark gave a sigh of relief as he hung up the phone.

He couldn't undo the damage to his relationship with Halley, but he could do what he was trained to do. First and last, he was a doctor.

The door banged against the wall. Mark turned, stone-faced, and saw Martha pushing Jill into the room.

"Jill has something to tell you," Martha huffed. She elbowed Jill forward.

Sniffling, Jill said, "I lied. I honestly didn't know if Daniel had been drinking." Her blue eyes shimmered with tears. "And I lied about Daniel giving Halley the brush-off. Halley isn't the troublemaker. I am."

Emotionally frozen, Mark shook his head, then walked between the women. Jill hadn't told him anything that he shouldn't have known. Both he and Jill should get down on their knees, crawl to Halley and beg her forgiveness. But first, he had a responsibility to Jimmy.

"Daniel voluntarily removed himself from the Owens case. I'll be in surgery if I'm needed." With a purposeful stride, he walked out the lounge door.

"He isn't going after her," Jill muttered.

Martha glared at Jill, who was staring at the long sequined gown hanging in the open closet beside Halley's coat.

"He can't. Duty comes first around here."

"I'm going after her," Jill said, walking toward the closet.

"Don't you think you've done enough damage?"

Jill nodded. "I know I can't take back what I said, but Halley will understand why I did it. I have to make amends or I won't be able to live with myself."

"I could fire you for deserting your post," Martha threatened.

Jill shrugged. "I was looking for a job when I came to St. Michael's."

"If I was Halley, I wouldn't speak to you."

"But you aren't Halley." Jill slipped into her coat and gathered up Halley's clothes. She patted her coat pocket, searching for a tissue. Unable to find one, she reached into Halley's coat, feeling a small circular object in the corner of the deep pocket. She pulled it out and examined it.

"What'd you find?" Martha asked, drawing closer.

Jill laid the ring on the flat of her hand. "A kid's ring. Purple stone."

"Let me see." Martha slipped the ring on her forefinger and held it up to the light. She remembered

Halley laughing, telling her about the valuable purple diamond. "Make sure she gets this. It's important."

"Okay." Jill slipped it back into Halley's pocket.

"And Jill—" Martha's chin jutted forward pugnaciously. She didn't play matchmaker often. She refused to be cheated out of seeing the stars back in Halley's eyes and the smile back on Mark's face. "You make certain Halley is at the ball tonight or—"

"You'll give me my walking papers?" She hurt too much to smile, but Jill gave Martha a thumbs-up sign. "I'll do my best. And if I don't get her to come maybe I'll just quit myself."

Martha watched Jill stride toward the door. "Inconsiderate kids nowadays. Whatever happened to giving two weeks' notice?"

"Don't you want to get rid of me as fast as you can?"

"No," Martha blustered. "You think I can run this hospital by myself?"

Somehow knowing Martha still needed her nursing skills lifted Jill's spirits. She smiled slightly. "Yeah, Martha. I think you can run St. Michael's single-handedly."

Chapter Twelve

She didn't disappear into thin air!'' Jill frowned. One quick glance around the admissions office told her Halley wasn't there. She'd searched every floor of the hospital. ''Where can she be?''

Her crepe-soled shoes squeaked as she rushed through the revolving doors and stepped outside. She looked to the left, then to the right. Her blue eyes narrowed. On the corner of the block, a lone coatless figure sat on the bus bench, staring across the street into Forest Park as though it were a bright, summer day and she had nothing better to do than to soak up some sun.

Jill cupped her hands around her mouth and shouted, ''Halley!''

Halley's thoughts insulated her from her surroundings. She stared straight ahead, totally oblivious to the cold, the exhaust from the bus pulling away from the curb, the cars passing her, the blaring horns. Nothing penetrated her rock-hard shell of misery.

Her brain was numb. Self-righteousness coalesced with self-condemnation. Right mixed with wrong. Duty with negligence. Jumbled together, none of them made sense.

She'd been right to confront Jill, Martha and Mark with Daniel's violation of hospital rules. She condemned herself for hesitating. The day she'd suspected he'd been drinking, she should have said something.

Who would have believed her?

She was the new kid on the block. No one had confidence in her. No one would have believed her then, just as no one believed her now.

Mark should have believed me, she thought miserably.

Reporting Daniel had been her duty as a responsible nurse. Negligence on her part could have resulted in a crisis situation for Jimmy. She couldn't allow an innocent child to suffer for Daniel's negligence.

Mark had wanted proof. When she'd given him the facts, he'd twisted them until they sounded as if she was a demented fool babbling gibberish. Did he expect her to have certified documents, signed by Daniel, sealed and notarized?

He should have trusted me!

Distrust wasn't the reason she'd asked him if he'd like a drink back at his house. She'd known that he'd pass her little test with flying colors. Her method of easing them into a conversation about doctors drinking while on duty had failed miserably. He'd touched her; rational thought had fled and been replaced with desire. She should have explained, but his sarcasm had destroyed her defenses.

If he wanted to Mark could accuse her of insubordination for slapping him. Nothing he'd said warranted her striking him. Should he file a report, she'd have to admit to lambasting him because he called her sweetheart. Sweetheart. He'd made the endearment a blasphemy. A choking sound lodged in her throat.

Her verbal retaliation had bounced ineffectually off him. He really had been blind, deaf and heartless. He had to be blind not to see how much she loved him. He had been deaf to her pleas and heartless when he couldn't see how each cutting question he asked left her vulnerable and defenseless.

"Halley!" Jill wrapped Halley's coat around her shoulders, bending her stiff arms until they slid into the sleeves. "You're freezing! What are you trying to do? Catch pneumonia?" she scolded.

Raising her chin from her chest, Halley looked at her friend. Friend? Pain darkened her eyes. Jill had lied, betrayed her, created a chasm between Mark and herself.

"Leave me alone."

"I won't," Jill asserted, scared by the blue tinge of Halley's lips. Automatically she felt her pulse. Slow, she gauged, but within the normal range. Slinging the evening gown over one shoulder, she hefted Halley to her feet. "You're coming with me."

Halley balked as a bus pulled to the stop. The door swung back. Heat gushed out.

"Hey, ladies! Are you getting in or not?"

Jill grabbed Halley around the waist and hauled her up the steps.

"Where's your tokens?" the driver asked, shutting the doors.

Halley disregarded the squabble taking place between Jill and the bus driver. Huddled into the corner of the front seat, she shivered. She turned her head toward the window.

As the bus pulled away from the curb, Halley closed her eyes and sent a silent prayer heavenward. Please, please, God, take care of Jimmy. Let him live. Guide the surgeon's hands. Make me be wrong about Daniel.

Her hands knotted together helplessly, the knuckles white from the cold. She remembered how despondent Mark had been when Jimmy had been taken to intensive care. In her heart she knew Mark might distrust her, hate her, but he'd investigate her claim. Right or wrong, he'd make certain Jimmy Owens received the best of care.

Jill put her arm across the back of the seat and hugged Halley. "I'm sorry."

Unyielding, Halley leaned away from her.

"Spit in my eye if it'll make you feel better. I deserve it."

Halley brushed aside Jill's hand from her shoulder.

"We're going to ride this bus until you thaw out and listen to me."

"You're wasting your breath," Halley managed to whisper through chattering teeth.

"I'm an expert at wasting my breath. For weeks I've been hassling Daniel. Remember my telling you that some men were worth rehabilitation? I think he's one of them." Jill dug a woolen scarf from her coat pocket and wrapped it around Halley's neck. "All his bravado and machismo is a mask he's hiding behind."

Listening to Jill extol Daniel's virtues was the last thing Halley wanted to do. She had all she could do to keep from covering her ears.

"Daniel is human. He's scared like the rest of us. Insecure. Add intense stress to anxiety and you've got the perfect candidate for a nervous breakdown. You aren't going to agree, but I'm going to give Daniel credit for one thing...he could have alleviated his problem by taking a handful of tranquilizers, but he didn't. He could have taken uppers to get started in the morning and downers to keep himself from shaking. No one, not even you, would have suspected. You have to admit, drug addiction is a hazard in the medical profession. Daniel avoided the easy trap."

Halley couldn't feel any sympathy for Daniel at this point. "He's a doctor," she said finally.

"Yeah. We all know that doctors are immune to life's pressures," Jill replied, her sweet tone belying her sarcasm. "Daniel started with an occasional glass of white wine to help him unwind, and before he knew it a vicious cycle started. The alcoholic content of his drinks grew in direct proportion to the size of his problems. He drank to minimize his problems; his problems grew because he drank."

"Excuses, excuses," Halley muttered to keep Jill from plucking at her heartstrings. "We're all under stress."

"And we all cope with stress differently," Jill agreed. "Some people cope through physical exertion, jogging, racquetball, tennis, golf. A lot of stress is relieved simply by watching football players, or boxers, or wrestlers pound the hell out of each other." Jill shifted closer to Halley. "There are many means of escaping: listening to music, dancing, reading, sex. They all let us escape, if only for a moment, the pressures bearing down on us."

"Listen to yourself. You've given at least ten *healthy* ways Daniel could have alleviated his stress."

Jill tapped her forehead. "Up here we know how. But sometimes we don't listen to reason. We resort to the fastest means available. Alcohol is fast, easy. In my case, lying was a quick solution. I lied to myself. I lied to you and Mark to cover up for Daniel. I sincerely apologize for the hurt my lies caused you. I'll grovel on the floor of the bus to kiss your feet if you doubt my sincerity."

Halley grabbed Jill's arm when she started to slide to her knees. "Don't be ridiculous. Where's your pride?"

"It bit the dust when I involved you in my lies. I violated every rule in the book of friendship. I can't expect you to forget my taking advantage of you, but I'm hoping you'll forgive me."

Halley hesitated, giving her tender heart a chance to toughen up. It didn't. She was stuck being a softhearted, gullible fool. Wearing her heart on her sleeve was risky, but the likelihood of changing its location was remote. "I accept your apology."

"I won't make empty promises," Jill said. "I love Daniel. I believe in him. I can't run and hide. That, too, would be fast and easy. But I know it wouldn't solve the problem."

Halley glared icily at Jill. "You mean me when you're talking about running and hiding, don't you?"

"Yeah...and me, and the Millers, and Tony, and Mark, and...everybody. Don't feel as though you're the only person who runs away when the going gets tough. You had the courage to fight for your convictions, then you ran before you found out whether you won or lost."

An image of Mark's forbidding scowl flashed in Halley's mind. "I lost."

"Daniel removed himself from the Owens case. Mark is assisting in surgery. Otherwise, he'd have been the one sitting here."

He must have believed her! Her prayer for Jimmy had been partially answered. With Mark in the operating room Jimmy's chances for recovery increased.

For a scant second hope flared inside Halley. What were her chances? "Did he ask you to find me?"

Jill's eyes dropped to her lap. "He said..."

Hope died. "Don't protect me with a lie. It won't solve the problem between Mark and myself."

"No, he didn't tell me to find you. But you should have seen him," Jill implored on Mark's behalf. "He walked from the lounge looking like a zombie in shell shock."

"Deaf, blind and heartless?" Halley asked, remembering the harsh names she'd called him. She turned her palm upward. Their first meeting had been a milestone in their relationship. She'd wanted to wipe the smug look off his face when he'd told her that Halley rhymes with alley, as in alley cat. She'd behaved like an alley cat, screeching and clawing.

"Worse." Jill brushed back the curtain of blond hair that had fallen forward. "I caused the dissension between the two of you. I knew jealousy would make him cross-eyed, unable to see anything straight."

"Mark? Jealous?" She shook her head in disbelief.

"Of course, he's jealous. My implying that you were chasing Daniel was a blow below the belt. It's obvious he's in love with you."

Halley clutched Jill's hand. "What makes you think he's in love with me?"

"Lord, woman, it's as plain as the nose on your face," Jill chided.

"No, it isn't, not to me. He hasn't told me he loves me."

"Haven't you noticed how he's changed? Nothing like being in love to alter a person's behavioral pattern."

"Mark treats me exactly the same as any other nurse," Halley argued, certain jealousy wasn't the reason behind his vicious questioning.

Jill chuckled. "He isn't the type of man who'd trap you in the broom closet for a bit of heavy necking. Haven't you noticed how he smiles at everyone? He used to be so stingy with his smiles that I thought he was hoarding them. Haven't you noticed the way his step has a springy bounce? How his eyes light up when he watches you with a patient?"

"Your imagination is playing tricks on you," Halley exclaimed while silently treasuring everything Jill said.

"I guess I've also imagined how you clam up when his name is mentioned. The reason behind your secretive little smile isn't too hard to figure out."

"Oh, Jill, I . . ." Her throat clogged when she thought of the spiteful things she'd said. "I . . . said terrible things to him."

"Unforgivable things?"

Halley nodded. "I told Mark that he and Oscar were alike. They both have eyes that don't see, ears that don't hear, and they're both heartless."

"So? Apologize."

"I can't."

"Why?"

"Because I meant every horrid word I said. I love him, but I'm not going to walk on eggshells for the rest of my life, waiting for him to explode because someone tells him a lie." Halley saw Jill's face blanch. "Don't blame yourself."

"Why not? I'm responsible for the rift between you and Mark."

Halley turned toward the window. The next bus stop was hers. She bundled herself together, dreading the cold.

"Jason's lies kept us apart initially, but there comes a time when hearing a lie shouldn't matter."

Jill agreed, but stipulated, "Confidence and trust open the eyes and ears. They make the heart listen." She stood. Reaching to the seat behind them, she picked up Halley's evening dress. "You're a giver, Halley. Sometimes you have to take. Grab what you want and hang on to it. That's what I'm doing with Daniel. I want him for keeps. He's less than perfect, but I love him. And I'm willing to fight to get him."

"The turnaround point for the bus is two blocks from here." Halley took the plastic-covered dress. "Thanks for coming after me ... friend."

As the bus slowed to a stop, Halley hugged Jill.

"Mark will be late picking you up tonight," Jill said, watching Halley keep her balance, weaving her way toward the exit. Grinning, Jill added, "Martha will skin him alive if he doesn't show up at the dance with you on his arm."

With a small wave, Halley stepped from the bus into the slush beside the curb. "She'd better sharpen her tomahawk," Halley said.

During the short, slippery hike to her apartment, Halley firmed her resolve. The whole bunch of them, Jill, Martha and Mark, could sit on her head and pound sand into her ears, but she wouldn't apologize for doing what she considered to be right.

Halley unlocked her door and entered her apartment. From habit, she crossed to the recorder on the phone, rewound the tape and punched the button to play the messages. She wondered if she should bother getting ready for the dinner dance.

"Halley." Her ears perked up as she recognized Mark's deep voice. "I'll be late, but I'll be there."

"Halley." Martha's voice was equally distinctive. "Don't be stubborn as a Missouri mule. You take a bubble bath, relax, then slip your bod into the dress I hemmed. Don't bother calling back. I'll see you at the dance ... with Mark."

Bod? Body? Martha's efforts to keep current with her son's slang never failed to make Halley smile.

She clicked the machine off. Her heart pounded. Butterflies fluttered in her stomach. In the heat of an-

1. How do you rate: _____
   (Please print book TITLE)

   1.6 ☐ excellent   .4 ☐ good   .2 ☐ not so good
   .5 ☐ very good   .3 ☐ fair   .1 ☐ poor

2. How likely are you to purchase another book:
   in this *series*?   by this *author*?
   2.1 ☐ definitely would purchase   3.1 ☐ definitely would purchase
   .2 ☐ probably would purchase   .2 ☐ probably would purchase
   .3 ☐ probably would not purchase   .3 ☐ probably would not purchase
   .4 ☐ definitely would not purchase   .4 ☐ definitely would not purchase

3. How does this book compare with romance books you usually read?
   4.1 ☐ far better than others   .4 ☐ not as good
   .2 ☐ better than others   .5 ☐ definitely not as good
   .3 ☐ about the same

4. Please check the statements you feel best describe this book.
   5 ☐ Realistic conflict   18 ☐ Too many foreign/unfamiliar words
   6 ☐ Too much violence/anger   19 ☐ Couldn't put the book down
   7 ☐ Not enough drama   20 ☐ Liked the setting
   8 ☐ Especially romantic   21 ☐ Made me feel good
   9 ☐ Original plot   22 ☐ Heroine too independent
   10 ☐ Good humor in story   23 ☐ Hero too dominating
   11 ☐ Not enough humor   24 ☐ Unrealistic conflict
   12 ☐ Not enough description of setting   25 ☐ Not enough romance
   13 ☐ Didn't like the subject   26 ☐ Too much description of setting
   14 ☐ Fast paced   27 ☐ Ideal hero
   15 ☐ Too predictable   28 ☐ Slow moving
   16 ☐ Heroine too juvenile/weak/silly   29 ☐ Not enough suspense
   17 ☐ Believable characters   30 ☐ Liked the subject

5. What aspect of the story outline on the back of the cover appealed to
   you most?
   31 ☐ location   32 ☐ subject
   33 ☐ characters   34 ☐ element of suspense in plot
   35 ☐ description of conflict

6. Did you feel this story was:
   36.1 ☐ too sexy
   .2 ☐ just sexy enough
   .3 ☐ not too sexy

7. Please indicate how many romance paperbacks you read in a month.
   37.1 ☐ 1 to 4   .2 ☐ 5 to 10   .3 ☐ 11 to 15   .4 ☐ more than 15

8. Please indicate your sex and age group.
   38.1 ☐ Male   39.1 ☐ under 18   .3 ☐ 25-34   .5 ☐ 50-64
   .2 ☐ Female   .2 ☐ 18-24   .4 ☐ 35-49   .6 ☐ 65 or older

9. Have you any additional comments about this book?
   (40)_____
   (41)_____
   (42)_____
   (43)_____
   _____
   _____

TABCDEFG

Thank you for completing and returning this questionnaire.

PRINTED IN U.S.A.

NAME _____
          (Please Print)
ADDRESS _____
CITY _____
ZIP CODE _____

BUSINESS REPLY MAIL

FIRST CLASS   PERMIT NO. 717   BUFFALO, NY

POSTAGE WILL BE PAID BY ADDRESSEE

NATIONAL READER SURVEYS

901 Fuhrmann Blvd.
P.O. Box 1395
Buffalo, N.Y. 14240-9961

ger, Mark had broken their date. What made him change his mind? Martha?

Shaking her head, she silently answered her question. Martha was persuasive, but Mark Abraham wouldn't be pushed into doing anything he didn't want to do. For whatever reason, Mark wanted to escort her to the dinner dance. The knowledge put wings on her feet.

She draped her dress on the bed, then dashed into the bathroom to start running water in the tub. Putting it in Martha's vernacular, tonight she'd have Mark's eyeballs poppin'. She'd hold her head high. She wouldn't run this time. Quite literally, she'd face the music...and dance.

Mark straightened his black bow tie in the rearview mirror. It took two tries. His hands shook nervously. The arrogant message he'd left on Halley's recorder should have been delivered in Oscar's voice. His self-confidence was at a record low.

"Damned cowlick!" He weighted the errant lock down with his hand, muttering, "I look like a penguin who's been plugged into an electrical transformer." For good measure, he added truthfully, "And I feel like a ten-year-old going on a date with a Hollywood starlet."

As Mark resigned himself to his appearance and opened the car door, he'd have given the contents of his billfold for an Alka Seltzer.

Carefully, he pushed his cashmere coat aside and pulled a long florist box from the back seat. He closed the car door and briskly strode toward Halley's door, the humble apology he'd practiced wedged between his teeth.

Beneath the porch light, Mark made a final check. His starched, pleated, white shirt stuck out above his black satin cummerbund. Mark shifted the long box under his arm and shoved the offensive shirt back into his pants. His unruly forelock fell forward. He raked it back. Drops of melted snow marred his highly polished shoes. Shifting from one foot to the other, he wiped the tip of each on the back of his trousers. Clearing his throat, he pressed the doorbell.

Her nerves shot, Halley jumped. The dangling earring she'd been in the process of inserting into the lobe of her ear slithered between her clumsy fingers. It clattered onto the mirrored dresser tray. Breathing hard, she shouted, "Coming," as the bell pealed again.

Had she taken the time for a final glance, she would have been pleased with her chic appearance. Strapless, the bodice of her sequined purple dress accentuated her full breasts. The clinging fabric hugged her slender waist and hips, emphasizing her womanly curves. Slit at the side from ankle to midthigh, the dress revealed tantalizing glimpses of her shapely legs as she walked to the door.

"Don't apologize," she mumbled, certain the pep talk she'd given herself while luxuriating in the tub would be forgotten the instant she opened the door.

She paused at the door long enough to quell the urge to throw it open, fling herself into Mark's arms and beg to be loved. No, she warned herself. Her hand wavered over her stomach, then smoothed the seams of her dress. Taking a deep breath to sustain herself, she opened the door.

He's so handsome, she thought.

She's incredibly beautiful, he realized as soon as he saw her.

Frigid night air rushed past Halley. Her violet eyes drank in the sight of Mark in full formal dress. Her fingers itched to have the right to brush across his clean-shaven cheek and linger in the dark lock of hair falling forward on his wide brow. His tuxedo called her attention to the width of his shoulders, the narrowness of his hips and the length of his muscular legs. The breath she'd been holding escaped through her lips in a heartfelt sigh.

Mark stood statuelike. He'd always known she was beautiful, but that word was inadequate to describe the way Halley looked tonight. Stunning, magnificent, glamorous would be more appropriate. He clenched his teeth. His arm tightened, crushing the slender box under his arm. His eyes dropped to her toes, his mind racing beneath the slightly parted slash.

He swallowed his rehearsed speech and pulled the smashed box from under his arm. "Here."

"Thanks." Her mouth and feet weren't receiving communication from her brain. She told her feet to move, her mouth to ask him inside.

"Ready?"

"Yeah." She stepped forward.

"Coat?"

Halley blinked. Coat? The temperature was below freezing, but she hadn't noticed. The tiny flames she'd seen dancing in the depths of Mark's dark eyes had warmed her.

"Oh, yes." In a daze, she turned toward the front closet. She set the box on the entry table. "Come in."

"Thanks."

His eyes followed the sway of her hips as she moved away from him. He nodded as he remembered her telling him to go to hell. *Well, ol' buddy, you've arrived.* It was agonizing being close enough to smell the fragrance she'd dabbed behind her ears without being able to taste her natural sweetness. It was agonizing wanting to touch her, but knowing she'd slap his face if he dipped his fingers into the shadow between her breasts. And it was sheer torture wanting to tell her how much he loved her, but strangling on the words.

"You look..." *Ravishing. Fantastic.* Overblown, corny superlatives, clung to the tip of his tongue. "...nice."

"You, too."

Disappointed by his unenthusiastic comment, she wondered if he hated her dress. Nice is such an insipid word, she thought. Nice day. Nice manners. Nice girl. She could hardly place that in Martha's poppin'-eyes category.

What about you? she asked herself. You haven't exactly been a silver-tongued vixen. Say something... anything... preferably something an addle-pated numbskull wouldn't say.

"Jimmy okay?" Glib, she thought, real quality small talk. She removed her white coat with the fox collar from the closet as she glanced over her shoulder. Mark stood behind her, as animated as Frosty the Snowman.

"He's stable." Which is more than you can say for yourself. Find a chair before your knees buckle and you thoroughly disgrace yourself. "Mind if I sit?"

Halley nodded her head, certain the gesture caused pea-sized pebbles to rattle around in the vacuum of her skull. "I'll put the flowers in a vase."

Mark folded himself into a corner of the sofa. Once she'd left the room his libido calmed down enough for him to say, "Halley, I owe you an apology."

She bit her lip to keep from replying, "I'm sorry, too." She ran cold water over her wrist into the vase.

"I'd heard the rumors about Daniel, but I didn't want to believe them. I kept reminding myself that you transferred from ER to get away from the whispers." His canned speech wasn't eliciting any response. He propped his elbows on his knees and ran his fingers through his hair. *You've given her the excuse, now give her the truth!* "You did the right thing by bringing Daniel's drinking problem to Martha's attention— eventually to my attention." *Damned coward!* He laced his hands together. "Plain and simple? While I was conducting a modern-day version of the Spanish Inquisition, I was jealous."

Tears dropped from Halley's eyes onto the fragile rosebuds nestled in angel's breath and fern fronds. She'd promised not to be reduced to tears, but his eloquent apology shook her to the core.

Mark cocked his head toward the kitchen. Had she heard him over the sound of the water splashing in the sink? He stumbled to his feet, uncertain his rubbery legs would carry him the short distance.

His heart hammered when he saw her silently crying, her face buried in the red roses.

In a flash he crossed the room and pulled her into his arms. "Don't cry, sweetheart. Don't cry." His lips moved against her dark curly hair. "It's my fault. I'm a fool for hurting you. I kept hearing what Jill said and...I guess I went a little crazy at the thought of you and Daniel being together."

Halley dug her fingers into his satin lapel. "I love you, Mark. I love you. Don't you know you're ten times the man that Daniel is?"

He lifted her chin with his thumb, gently wiping her tears with his fingertips. Sweet, pure joy pulsed through him. "I love you, sweetheart. Forgive me?"

Halley could hear her heart singing, "I love you, sweetheart." The melodic phrase accompanied by his impassioned apology made tears of happiness glisten in her eyes.

"Oh, Mark, I could forgive you anything as long as you love me." The truth of her vow shone in her eyes. He sealed her promise with a kiss. Silently he swore he'd keep a tight rein on his jealousy. Halley was as spectacular as her namesake. A man had to be strong to capture a comet and hold it in his hands.

Chapter Thirteen

Do you have anything underneath this dress?'' Mark whispered. His hands had thoroughly explored her back searching for a crease of some sort to disprove his theory.

Secure in the warmth of his love, she quipped naughtily, "There's only a twelve-inch zipper between knowing and wondering."

"Sweetheart," he groaned, imagining the wide bed with clean, crisp lilac-colored sheets that beckoned him. "We'll completely miss the dinner dance. We're already late."

Halley snuggled against him. "Late? That reminds me of something you ought to know. I bought one of those do-it-yourself kits. Negative results," she said, happy to report that her father wouldn't have to oil up the white shotgun. "Good news, huh?"

He hugged her tightly to still a voice from the past, a voice asking, Who'd want your child? Forcing himself to smile, he freed Halley. "We'd better make an appearance at the dance."

"A cameo appearance? You know, like the celebrities make on television. One minute you see them and the next they're gone."

He frowned at her impudent suggestion. "We're expected..."

He broke off in the middle of Cleo's favorite statement. Why was Cleo's ghost haunting him? He loved Halley. She loved him. There weren't any similarities between the past and the present.

"All right," Halley agreed with a sexy pout. "I expect a rain check on what your body language has been saying to me."

Elated, she interpreted his scowl as being directly related to their leaving when they both wanted to stay.

"I'll get your coat," Mark said, then gave her a quick, hard, unsatisfying kiss.

Laughter bubbled up from deep inside Halley. Tonight promised to be a night she'd remember forever.

During the ride to the Chase Hotel, she wickedly teased Mark by writing sexy little messages on his thigh.

"I think I'll drive this car until the tires fall off and the axle grinds into the pavement," Mark said as he helped her from the car.

"Why?" She batted her eyes with feigned innocence.

"Because, sweetheart, there are more memories locked in there than I had in my renovated '55 Chevrolet."

He gave her backside a playful swat. Then his hand moved possessively to her hip.

"Behave, Dr. Abraham," Halley scolded, her lilting voice filled with delight.

Mark caught the young valet staring at Halley. His grip tightened. The doorman smiled at her, and Mark's scowl deepened.

A sense of déjà vu twisted his stomach into a hard knot. Mark slowed his step as he had second thoughts about attending the annual social function. *Don't be a damned fool,* he thought. *She isn't like Cleo. It won't be the same.*

"I'll check your coat." Mark swallowed a low moan as he removed her wrap. He glanced at the men who were in the lobby.

All eyes were on her, sizing her up, wondering what the hell she was doing with him.

Halley pivoted, giving Mark a bright-eyed wink. "Wonder who Martha came with."

"Her son," Mark replied, his words clipped.

"Great. I've heard so much about him I can hardly wait."

A muscle along Mark's jaw twitched. "I'll be back in a moment. Why don't you go on in? I think I'll stop by the men's room."

"I don't mind waiting."

With a curt nod, Mark turned toward the coat-check room. His stomach threatened open rebellion. Physically ill at the prospect of enduring hours of watching other men fall all over Halley, he shoved the ticket into his pocket and hurried toward the men's room.

Halley's eyes narrowed as she watched Mark's retreat.

Intuitively, she knew something was wrong. From the instant he'd politely assisted her from the car, he'd become stiff and cold. She'd been kidding when she told him to behave. Surely he wasn't upset because of a playful taunt.

"Halley! You look terrific," Martha exclaimed enthusiastically, taking her by the hands and squeezing them tightly. "Is he with you?" she whispered.

Pushing aside her apprehensive feelings, Halley grinned at Martha. "Who?"

"Santa Claus," Martha wisecracked.

Halley wrinkled her nose. "He's busy loading the sleigh."

"How'd you like to work Christmas Day, New Year's Eve, Valentine's Day..."

"Uncle! I surrender." Her violet eyes twinkled with merriment. "Mark is my escort."

Martha's wire-framed glasses slipped off the bridge of her nose. Grinning at her successful debut as matchmaker of the century, she barely noticed.

"Your dress is beautiful," Halley said appreciatively. "Red velvet is gorgeous on you."

Martha preened, sucking in her ample waist. "Makes me feel like a cross between Mrs. Claus and a Coke machine, but I love it anyway." She turned toward the young man standing a few steps behind her. "Halley, this is my son, Christopher."

"Hubba-hubba-ding-ding! I thought all pediatric nurses wore orthopedic shoes."

Martha jabbed her glasses back in place. "Here I've been impressing Halley with my modern lingo and you came up with an expression that was before my time."

"Come on, Mom. You know it's every child's duty to make a liar out of their parents at every opportunity." He pulled his hand from behind his back and dangled a limp sprig of mistletoe over his mother's head. "Meat and potatoes first—" his head jerked in Halley's direction "—then scrumdilli-ious dessert."

The good-natured teasing between mother and son amused Halley. Christopher's silver tongue was typical of a handsome young man who thought he could conquer the world. Over Martha's shoulder, she saw Mark approaching them. At the same moment Christopher raised the mistletoe over her head.

"Close your eyes. Pretend I'm ten years older and fabulously wealthy," Christopher prompted roguishly.

Mark stopped dead in his tracks.

Halley instantly imagined a green light over Mark's head flickering in bold letters: jealous. She remembered hearing bitterness in his voice earlier that afternoon when he'd said, "Cleo told me I was ugly."

His brow furrowed. Lips thinning to a flat line, Mark reprimanded himself. *Don't be a fool. Martha's son is a kid, barely out of short pants. You can't go around passing out blinders to every man who gives Halley an appreciative look.*

Halley could see jealousy eating at him. He loved her, but he was scared to death of losing her love to another man. Before the night was over, she promised, she'd exorcise his doubts. The time had come to wage war against the insecurities Cleo had left in her wake.

Fight for him. Don't run and hide, she thought. Jill's words goaded her into action.

Lightly plucking the bedraggled twig from between Christopher's fingers she made a beeline toward Mark. Fortified by his love she stood on her toes, looped her arms around his neck and whispered, "I love you." She brushed her lips across his with a kiss fraught with meaning. "Only you."

"Hey! You forgot to hold the mistletoe over his head," Christopher protested.

"We don't need mistletoe," she said for Mark's ears alone. "We only need each other. Come dance with me. I want to hold you."

Mark felt the heavy weight of gloom lifting from his shoulders. She'd saved him from near disaster. He stood a bit taller. He waved at Martha, then led Halley to the small parquet dance floor cleared in the center of the ballroom.

Slow, dreamy music drifted around them. Halley laid her head against his shoulder. His hands spanned her waist and settled on her hips. Soon they were moving together as one.

Mark shut his eyes for a moment. He felt her fingers working the tenseness from his shoulder muscles. His thighs skimmed intimately against her. Gradually he began to relax.

Halley took a page from Martha's book and dared to go where angels feared to tread. "I'm not Cleo."

"I know, sweetheart."

They swayed in rhythm to the music, barely moving their feet.

"It wasn't just Jason's lies that kept us apart, was it?"

"No."

"Are you jealous of Jason?"

"No. I could cheerfully throttle him for being abusive to you, but I wouldn't be any more jealous of him than I am of Martha's kid."

Halley felt as though she were an amateur burglar picking a complicated lock. She could hear the steady thud of his heart as the tumblers began to fall. Be careful, she warned herself. One wrong word and he'd lock her out of his heart.

"Do you believe me when I tell you that I love you?"

"Hmm." His brows knitted in concentration. *Ask her why she loves you. Why she'd choose you over every available man in the room.*

Halley was certain Mark wasn't aware of his arm muscles constricting. Although he continued to hold her at a respectable distance, his fingers dug into her flesh.

She had to know what he was thinking. Leaning toward him, she tilted her head back until their eyes met. "Talk to me, Mark. I'm afraid of asking the wrong question. I feel like I'm blindfolded, probing around your heart to remove an elusive ache. Help me, please."

Mark winced. She was so close, so vulnerable, so loving. Why couldn't he share the secret he'd kept buried since Cleo shattered his self-confidence? Halley loved him. She was begging him to bare his soul to her. Why couldn't he?

Because understanding was beyond her comprehension, he told himself. No woman, regardless of her compassionate nature, could be expected to understand how a man felt when he walked into a room with a gorgeous woman on his arm and found most of the men in the room stripping her with their eyes; or how it felt to know that the moment his back was turned another man would be closing in on his territory; or the horrendous doubt that could build when the woman he loved was several minutes late.

Mark knew he wasn't the only man who suffered from the demons of jealousy. He'd talked to other men married to beautiful women. They, too, felt diminished by their wives' physical beauty.

He'd heard several of the men say, "If I could live my life over, I'd marry a homely woman. You know where you stand with them. They take care of you instead of the other way around."

Some of the men had been fathers, and those who were, felt lucky that their wives had consented to have children. One man admitted to tricking his wife into a "surprise" pregnancy by telling her he was sterile.

Cleo had been smart. She had known precisely what she wanted and what she was willing to give. Money and social position had been her top priorities. Children were her last priority. They weren't part of her plans.

Halley had proven she was different from Cleo, but Halley had been mighty pleased to inform him that the rabbit hadn't died. Rabbit, hell. The strip of paper hadn't turned blue. Medical research had saved the rabbits.

His thoughts digressed as the five-piece orchestra weaved another popular tune into their medley.

He loved Halley. In bed, she was the stuff men fantasized over. Right now, Halley flowed over him like warm honey. Through her sequined dress he could feel her breasts press against his chest. With his eyes closed, he could imagine how lovely they were.

Mark swallowed. To explain his feelings would be pointless. Given the knowledge, she couldn't change anything. He'd accept her love, but he knew it would have to be on a temporary basis. When she found another man who was handsome and clever, she'd eventually leave him. The thought of Halley with another man better than himself made him physically ill.

Purposely, he widened the space between them.

"The song is ending. I need a little breathing space or I'll embarrass you."

His meaning was perfectly obvious, but Halley clung tightly to him, reluctant to permit even a fraction of an inch between them. He smiled down at her, but his smile was forced, lifeless.

She'd seen his near-black eyes lit with passion, etched with weariness and suffering from pain. The urge to flee to a small corner of the world and take him with her left her unable to return his smile.

"Mark, please, whatever it is you're hiding, you've got to tell me."

Masking his thoughts, he blew lightly into the ringlets of curls around her ear. "Lust, my dear," he teased in a spooky voice.

"Bull-roar."

Nodding his head, Mark agreed. "Yes, they do."

"I'm not going to be a straight man for a comedy routine." Her chin thrust upward stubbornly.

"I have it on the best authority that bulls do roar. They occasionally toss in a few grunts and snorts, but they... Ouch!"

Halley's heel bore down on his instep hard enough for him to notice, but not hard enough to really hurt him. "I know good and well there's a reason for your jealousy. So help me, I'm going to ask each person in this ballroom if they've been introduced to the green-eyed monster on your shoulder," she huffed. "And what they know about his background."

"You're inviting strangers to bend your ear with rumors and lies." He faked a yawn to hide his concern.

"It has something to do with Cleo, doesn't it?"

Mark raised his hand to the back of her neck. "Cleo isn't here. She spends Christmas in Bermuda."

"How can we build a permanent relationship..." She watched him raise one eyebrow. "That's it, isn't it? You love me, but you're too scared of failure to make a commitment."

Mark forced himself to chuckle. "You're like a pint-size bulldog tenaciously sniffing the wrong trail."

"You'll marry me?" she blurted impulsively, speaking before thinking.

"Is that a proposal?"

Grab for the brass ring. Be a taker for a change. Halley smiled. "Why not?"

"Why?" Mark countered. He trusted Halley and could ask her the one question he'd been unable to ask Cleo. It was better to know now than suffer later.

Deliberately Jill bumped against Halley's shoulder as the music began to fade.

"Halley! I've been looking everywhere for you." Jill's left hand fluttered between Mark and Halley. "You didn't catch a cold this afternoon, did you?"

Too polite to tell Jill to buzz off, Halley answered, "No. I'm fine." Her short reply bordered on being rude. She was right in the middle of discussing marriage with the man she loved. Jill's timing couldn't have been worse.

Jill ran her forefinger over the arch of her brow, then scratched the tip of her nose. "Lavish party, isn't it?"

Halley glanced around the dimly lit room. She'd barely noticed the fountain on the linen-covered buffet table, or the carved-ice swan spouting champagne, or the twinkling lights overhead. "Yes."

Daniel appeared and, taking Jill's hand, he held it in front of Halley's nose. "Notice the ring before my fiancée starts picking her teeth, would you?"

Before Halley could glance at the engagement ring, Jill grabbed her and hugged her, jumping up and down. "Isn't it wonderful? I'm so happy I could die! Daniel decided to make his temporary leave of absence our honeymoon! We're going to Egypt to climb the pyramids and swim in the Nile. Isn't that the most romantic thing you've ever heard of? And I owe it all to you, my friend."

Well-wishers overheard Jill and gathered around the foursome. Halley heard Mark offer his congratulations to Daniel.

For a plug nickel Halley would have told everyone she'd proposed to Mark and was impatiently awaiting his reply. She had the gumption, but not the will. First she had to ferret out the reason behind Mark's reservations.

Halley smiled as though cued, but she was barely aware of the crowd of people around her. Mark was from the Show Me state, but even for a Missourian he was amazingly difficult to convince. No matter, she thought. She had every intention of proving to him that they could be as happy as Jill and Daniel.

Chapter Fourteen

Why? Why do you want to marry me?

Halley pondered his question as she edged away from the group of well-wishers. Finding the right answer would be as difficult as being a specialist at the Atlanta Disease Control Center who was confronted with a rare fatal disease. The specialist would have to interpret test information, then prescribe treatment based on the patient's description of myriad aches and pains.

A careful examination and analysis of the facts was of vital importance before answering his complex, single-word question: why? She had two facts to consider. One, he was jealous. Two, he had a nasty case of the "uglies," thanks to Cleo.

Was there a third problem afflicting Mark? One that linked the other two together?

Passing near a group of ER doctors and nurses, Halley smiled, but kept moving toward the banquet table. She cast a furtive glance over her shoulder to locate Mark. His eyes followed her path, but to the unsuspecting doctor talking to him, Mark appeared to be clinging to each profound phrase he uttered. As inconspicuously as possible, she pointed toward the food-laden table. Mark gave a sharp nod to indicate he'd received her silent communication.

Preoccupied, Halley picked up a small china plate and selected gourmet hors d'oeuvres at random. While her plate quickly filled, her mind came up empty in its search for the third problem. She strolled toward a line of vacant seats secluded by several potted palms.

Whatever the mysterious problem was, Mark had it buried deep inside of him and was unwilling to reveal it. She'd poked and pried by asking direct questions, but in the final analysis, he'd given her almost no information.

Seating herself, she nibbled some pâté de foie gras. She'd eaten half of it before realizing the paste made from goose livers wasn't quiche. She forced herself to swallow the loathsome mixture.

With apprehension she eyed the remaining food on her plate. The thin crackers she'd covered with cream cheese and miniature blueberries looked decidedly suspicious. Raising one to her mouth, she sniffed before tasting. It smelled salty. Her plebeian taste buds recoiled. Caviar—sturgeon eggs. Turning up her nose, she set the plate aside. She'd stick to food served from plastic pouches.

So, *Nurse* Twain, she asked herself as she looked across the room at Mark. Will your caring, sympathetic hands be sufficient treatment to cure the two problems diagnosed?

Dancing with Mark was Band-Aid treatment for his jealousy. Two aspirin, a warm bath and plenty of bed rest would have been as effective—as long as she shared the bath and bed. Unfortunately, she couldn't spend her life squeaky clean between his sheets. She smiled, almost wishing that remedy were realistic enough to try.

No, extreme caution was warranted, at least until he felt secure in her love. She'd convince him that he was the only man she loved. Her natural tendency to be affectionate would make this phase of his treatment thoroughly enjoyable.

His self-perception problem stymied her. How could she make Mark aware of his charisma? When he spoke, people listened. The entire nursing staff, single and married, young and old, had placed Dr. Abraham on a mile-high pedestal. A conceited man or a man with solid self-esteem would have to squeeze his head with both hands to get through the double doors at St. Michael's. Admittedly, Mark wasn't a Robert Redford look-alike, but he was miles away from scaring innocent virgins in the dark, too.

Mark shaved every morning. Couldn't he see his reflection in the mirror? She shook her head. Obviously, Cleo had managed to cloud his image of himself.

Love and affection, she mused wryly, were standard treatment for a lovesick illness. She could provide that medicine easily. Her optimism ebbed as she realized she'd already given him a strong dose of both of them. Love and affection put his illness in remission, but they weren't a cure.

She was back where she started from. She'd tried to pick the lock, tried to open it with two keys, but she'd failed. A niggling suspicion that she had the third key and didn't know it bothered her. Sometime during the past weeks, he'd given her the key and she'd tucked it into the back of her mind as being unimportant.

Strains of "Bewitched, Bothered and Bewildered" brought Halley to her feet. Had she whispered the song title into the orchestra leader's ear, she couldn't have chosen a more appropriate tune.

Raising on tiptoe to see above the heads of the guests gravitating toward the dance floor, she strained to catch a glimpse of Mark. She spotted him near the entrance, deep in conversation with the kidney specialist on the Jimmy Owens case. Not wanting to intrude, she moved toward him at a leisurely pace, hoping he'd notice her and end the conversation.

Mark caught sight of Halley. Merely watching her walk toward him accelerated his heart rate. She was a rare beauty, beautiful inside and outside.

"Yes," Mark agreed, only half listening to what Jimmy's specialist had said. "Would you excuse me?"

He'd barely reached her side when he heard the beeper he'd clipped on his waistband signal him. Halley smiled when she saw several nearby doctors grimace, then grin abashedly, each relieved that the beeping sound wasn't coming from his beeper.

"Duty calling?" Halley asked, tucking her hand in the crook of his arm.

"Yes, but you don't have to leave. I'll arrange for Martha or..."

"I'm coming with you, Dr. Abraham." She stroked the underside of his jacket sleeve. "There isn't anyone I'd rather be with than you."

His special smile told Halley she'd administered the correct dosage of affection.

"I'll call the answering service from the lobby."

"Give me the cloakroom ticket and I'll pick up my coat while you're calling," Halley replied, reverting to the role of an efficient nurse. "I'll meet you at the front door."

Minutes later, the valet opened the passenger's door of the Mercedes for Halley. Gracefully holding her gown, she slid into the seat. Mark's frown was back in place.

"Emergency case?"

"Neonate. Streptococcus gone bad," Mark said, accelerating as he made a sharp turn. His rear tires squealed on the dry pavement.

Infant with pneumonia. Halley silently translated his medical jargon. "Clinical manifestations?"

"Lethargic, distended abdomen, respiration irregular, dehydrated. ER is taking the culture specimens I ordered."

"Good thing the Chase Park Plaza is close to the hospital," Halley murmured, concerned.

"It would be better if the organizers of the banquet provided for a police escort. I've yet to attend one of these shebangs when one of us didn't have to leave early."

Mark swerved into a reserved parking space near the emergency entrance.

"You go ahead. I'll be right behind you," Halley said, knowing he could be with the patient sooner if he wasn't matching her high-heeled gait.

He was inside the hospital before she'd located the door latch. Fleet of foot, she mused, wondering if sprinting had been part of Mark's medical training. Right now she'd give just about anything for her orthopedic shoes.

Automatic doors swooshed open in front of her. Familiar with the ER setup, she crossed to the admission desk.

"Hi, Halley," Stephanie Joskey greeted. "Missing the fast pace of ER so soon? Want to transfer back?"

"No, to both questions, Steph." She glanced around, locating the parents of the baby, who were being comforted by a nurse whom Halley recognized. "Dr. Abraham run through here?"

"Yeah. They're taking the baby to the isolation room on pediatrics." Her voice dropped to a low whisper. "First-time parents are a nervous wreck with new infants. Ampicillin, oxygen, and IV and twenty-four hours at St. Michael's will convince them of the miracles of modern medicine."

Relieved, Halley grinned. "I think I'll go up to pediatrics."

"You on night duty?" Stephanie teased. "I heard they were spiffy dressers up there, but I didn't realize working in pediatrics required formal attire."

Spinning on one foot Halley quipped, "Now you know why there's a waiting list for nurses wanting a transfer."

"Does the hospital issue cute little purple nurses' caps?"

"Dozens," Halley called softly over her shoulder. Hospital etiquette frowned on boisterous joking between the nurses. "With matching sequins."

Smiling, Halley entered the elevator, pushed the button and waited for the door to reopen. Seconds later, she stepped into the corridor feeling at home in the familiar surroundings.

"He's in the isolation room," the records clerk said, matching Mark's tuxedo with Halley's long dress.

"I won't go in. I'll watch through the window."

Halley slipped off her high heels, picked them up, lifted her dress to keep it from tripping her and silently walked down the hallway.

A long, narrow, vertical window allowed Halley to watch Mark.

Both doctor and nurse wore masks. Although she couldn't hear what was being said, she knew Mark was murmuring softly to the child. His capable hands were firm but gentle as he placed the infant in the oxygen tent. While the nurse adjusted the IV, Mark glanced toward the door.

Her eyes met his and held for one heartrending moment.

Halley gasped. In her mind's eyes she could see Mark solemnly handing her the golden key.

Her mouth scarcely moved as she whispered, "He wants children." The key turned. "Beautiful babies."

Knees shaking, Halley braced herself against the door, her hand pressed against the window. Unnoticed, her shoes dropped from her hand. Her eyes closed.

She recalled smugly telling Mark she wasn't pregnant. While she had been afraid of trapping him by getting pregnant, he'd been holding his breath and praying she was carrying his child.

When her eyes fluttered open, Mark stood on the opposite side of the windowpane. His hand paired with hers.

"I love you, Mark," she whispered with full meaning.

"And I love you, sweetheart."

Halley stepped backward as Mark pushed the door ajar. "I'm ready."

Oh Lord, so am I.

In companionable silence they walked from the pediatric wing of the hospital to the car.

He'd read her lips through the door window of the isolation room. Without Mark having to bare his soul, Halley knew he wanted children. Had she found the idea abhorrent, she would have fled. Instead, she'd stood tall, resolute, and candidly said, "I love you, Mark."

Months from now, she wouldn't ridicule him as Cleo had. She wanted him. She loved him. She wanted his babies.

His topsy-turvy world had righted itself. Halley understood him. She accepted his love of medicine as being an essential part of him. Duty would often come first, but Halley would be by his side, helping and supporting him.

Without being aware of it, she'd answered his question, told him *why* she loved him. A woman married a man for love, commitment and the joy of raising children. He remembered Halley saying she wanted the impossible dream. He would do everything within his power to make the dream a reality.

On the way to her apartment Halley cuddled close to Mark. Anxious to rid him of any mistaken ideas, she said, "I'm going to pitch that charming little protective device the gynecologist gave me."

"Hmm?" His lips barely curved.

"You're going to have to marry me."

"Uh-huh." His grin became a smile.

"I'm not going to be an unwed mother."

"Right." His smile widened.

"We're going to elope—immediately."

Mark chuckled. "Okay."

Frustrated by his agreeable grunts, Halley nudged him in the ribs with her elbow. His heartwarming smile wasn't enough. "Talk to me!"

"Nope."

"Why not?"

Mark pulled the car to the curb.

"Why are you stopping three blocks from my apartment?"

"Because, sweetheart, we're going to talk." His laughter mingled with hers as he turned her to face him.

"You're parked in a bus zone."

"Doctors have immunity with the police department."

"Oh?" she murmured skeptically.

"Has anyone told you that when you're slightly miffed your cheeks turn bright pink, those violet eyes of yours twinkle and those short breaths make your breasts..." His thumb skated into the shadow of her cleavage.

"Mark!" she protested, pushing against his chest, certain a cop was going to tap on the window.

"I'm not deaf," he said, chuckling. "But there are certain advantages to being blind. I'd love to braille you." He covered her hand, which was over his heart. "Feel it."

Halley grinned, realizing he was proving to her that he wasn't heartless, or deaf, or blind. "You're no dummy, either."

"Do you want to talk or test my lips to see if they're smear-proof?"

"Talk." She folded her arms across her chest. "One of us needs a lesson in genetics."

"Genetics?"

"Correct, Doctor. Basic genetics. Dark hair from my father. Eye color from my mother. Petiteness from my maternal grandmother. I wasn't given genetic choices. They happened. DNA."

Mark twirled a lock of her hair between his thumb and forefinger. "In your case, DNA stands for Damned Nice Anatomy."

"For your information, fighting off unwanted passes isn't my idea of a wonderful pastime. Nor is having to bend over backward before another woman sees me as anything other than competition."

His fingers ceased moving. "I've never thought of beauty as being..."

"A handicap. Well, it can be. I'd rather be admired for what's up here—" she tapped her temple "—than what size bra I wear. Genetically speaking, *you* are the lucky one. You're intelligent, tall, well-built, and I think you're the most handsome man I know."

"You wouldn't lie about genetics, would you?"

"I don't lie, not even when telling the truth is difficult. Was it Mark Twain who said, 'Is Jack handsome? Don't ask Jill; she's in love.' To me, you're handsome. We'll make beautiful babies."

"Did Mark Twain really say that?"

"Yeah. I'll introduce him to you when we go visit my parents."

Quick on the uptake, Mark laughed. "You have a brother named Mark?"

"My dad is an avid reader of the real Mark Twain and my mother dabbles in astronomy."

"And their daughter believes in magical purple diamond rings and cries when she receives long-stemmed roses. I'm going to love your family."

"Soon we'll have our own family. You. Me. And a half-dozen little ones." She peppered kisses across the fine lines on his brows.

"Finished talking?" Mark asked, his voice husky with emotion.

Halley nodded, eager for his kisses.

"You're going to start something I won't be able to stop," Mark warned.

"We'll name our first child Mercedes," she teased as he started the car. "And the second, R. Royce, and the third, Lincoln, and the fourth, Bronco..."

COMING NEXT MONTH

VOYAGE OF THE NIGHTINGALE—Billie Green
Braving exotic poisons and native sacrifices, cultured Bostonian
Rachel McNaught scoured the tropics for her missing brother. But
what she found was ruffian sailor Flynn, who scorned her money...and
stole her heart.

SHADOW OF DOUBT—Caitlin Cross
Who *was* widow Julia Velasco? A decadent gold digger who'd kidnapped
her own son for profit? Or a desperate mother in need of protection?
Mesmerized by her, attorney Anson Wolfe sought the elusive truth.

THE STAR SEEKER—Maggi Charles
"Your lover will be tall, dark and handsome," the palm-reader told
her. But shopkeeper Hilary Forsythe was avoiding men—particularly
banker J.A. Mahoney, who handled her business loan...and mismanaged
her emotions!

IN THE NAME OF LOVE—Paula Hamilton
Madcap Samantha Graham was determined to join the CIA. Agent
Jim Collins was bedazzled but skeptical. To "protect" her from her
impulsive self, would he ruin her chances—in the name of love?

COME PRIDE, COME PASSION—Jennifer West
When Cade Delaney returned to Dixie, he had bitter revenge on his
mind. The object: proud Elizabeth Hart. The obstacle: his burning
passion for her.

A TIME TO KEEP—Curtiss Ann Matlock
Jason Kenyon was old enough to be Lauren Howard's father, but that
didn't stop them from falling in love. Could their precious time together
last...or would the odds against them tear them apart?

AVAILABLE THIS MONTH:

CRISTEN'S CHOICE
Ginna Gray

PURPLE DIAMONDS
Jo Ann Algermissen

WITH THIS RING
Pat Warren

RENEGADE SON
Lisa Jackson

A MEASURE OF LOVE
Lindsay McKenna

HIGH SOCIETY
Lynda Trent

FOUR UNIQUE SERIES
FOR EVERY WOMAN YOU ARE...

Silhouette Romance

Heartwarming romances that will make you
laugh and cry as they bring you all the wonder
and magic of falling in love.

6 titles
per month

Silhouette Special Edition

Expanded romances written with emotion and
heightened romantic tension to ensure
powerful stories. A rare blend of passion and
dramatic realism.

6 titles
per month

Silhouette Desire

Believable, sensuous, compelling—and
above all, romantic—these stories deliver
the promise of love, the guarantee
of satisfaction.

6 titles
per month

Silhouette Intimate Moments

Love stories that entice; longer, more
sensuous romances filled with adventure,
suspense, glamour and melodrama.

4 titles
per month

Silhouette Romances
not available in retail outlets in Canada

SIL-GEN-1A